ACCLAIM FOR

AFTER BIRTH

"Elisa Albert's brilliant new novel . . . wrenches out something so new we barely recognize it . . . Obscene, reckless, vicious, hilarious, and above all real. Albert has inherited the house Grace Paley built, with its narrow doorways just wide enough for wit and tragedy and blistering, exasperated love. And no one is better suited to manage that estate, to keep it unapologetically going, to keep its rooms of inquiry open . . . [*After Birth*] ought to be as essential as *The Red Badge of Courage*."

—Merritt Tierce, *New York Times Book Review*

"A novel that captures our time with bracing, propulsive energy and brilliant honesty . . . A deeply resonant and empathic reading experience . . . Albert is virtuosic . . . Her language takes the sentimental platitudes that all mothers are fed (lies!) and spits them back with purifying fury." —Jessica Roake, *Washington Post*

"Albert's scathing send-up of modern motherhood boils with dark humor and brutal honesty." —*People*

"Coarse and poetic and funny as hell, full of the hard truths no one tells you beforehand, including just that: No one tells you the truth." —Ellen Akins, *Star Tribune*

"Ari's voice is freewheeling, manic, edgy: the voice of an intelligent woman on the edge of a nervous breakdown. It's like Lorrie Moore but more cracked open, running on not enough sleep."

—Alexis Nelson, *Los Angeles Review of Books*

"Intelligent and painfully real . . . It's going to tear everything you thought about birth and motherhood to shreds."

—Jeva Lange, *Electric Literature*

"[A] wonderful primal howl of a novel."

—Sam Sacks, *Wall Street Journal*

"A smartly acerbic exploration of motherhood."

—Sarah Meyer, *O, The Oprah Magazine*

"An entertaining take on the vicissitudes of female friendship."
—Carmela Ciuraru, *New York Times*

"In *After Birth,* Albert turns her now-trademark dark humor and merciless lens on the first chapters of life from the perspective of a new mother, and the result is a perfect balance of light and dark." —Sarah Seltzer, *Lilith*

"By turns poetic, insightful, and deeply troubling, but always, always very honest." —Rebecca Vipond Brink, *The Frisky*

"Compelling and searing . . . Albert has given us a portrait of modern motherhood that will provide insight for some and provoke others. For others still, in its quieter moments, as it reaches for an honest way to talk about birth, it will be like that big old bell ringing in them, a reading process of recognition and reunion." —Rozalind Dineen, *Guardian*

"Screams with energy and sparkles with wit . . . *After Birth* lays bare one of the secrets of growing older, namely that the true fantasy of a woman no longer in her twenties is not for a man, but for a good friend." —Batya Ungar-Sargon, *Haaretz*

"Provocative and darkly humorous . . . What makes Ari such a compelling narrator is her willingness to say things that, spoken aloud, would merit permanent blacklisting by mommy groups everywhere . . . Her voice is one that we mothers desperately need to hear." —Isabelle FitzGerald, *Rumpus*

"There is vitality . . . a psychological candor that at once illuminates an extreme individual response and gives way to a sheltered aspect of the human condition. [Albert] achieves truth telling, as the great Norwegian novelist Knut Hamsun once cast it, in 'unselfish inwardness.'" —Minna Proctor, *Bookforum*

"As sharp as a fresh-cut diamond . . . Bright, angry, very funny, diving into uncomfortable truths about the female body and female behavior, this novel has it all." —*Flavorwire*

"Wildly insightful and hilarious." —Diana Spechler, *Slate*

"Ari's voice is ferociously funny, confrontational, and dark; Albert uses it to tackle feminism, Holocaust memory, inherited traumas, motherhood, and marriage."

—Catherine Carberry, *Paris Review*

"*After Birth*'s frank talk . . . would almost certainly have left Bukowski squicked out and quaking behind his hangover-sunglasses . . . Perhaps in all those conversations about likeable female characters, we've forgotten something key: Characters like Ari are only unlikeable if you've never talked to an actual woman . . . The anti-heroine I'd been waiting for."

—Megan Burbank, *Portland Mercury*

"Entertaining, funny, and heartfelt. And most importantly, Albert can write. She's clever and caustic, and her prose crackles with energy; sometimes something primal, sometimes slightly manic . . . One of the many refreshing things about *After Birth* is that fundamentally it's a book about relationships between women . . . Necessary and powerful."

—Lucy Scholes, *Independent*

"Manage[s] to take the temperature of the culture of modern motherhood to impressive effect . . . With shades of light and dark, *After Birth* is the unutterable misgivings of new motherhood writ large." —Tanya Sweeney, *Irish Independent*

"Intense and darkly comic, Albert's novel offers a refreshingly frank account of life." —*Ms.* magazine

"[A] cri de coeur . . . Albert imbues [Ari] with searing honesty and dark humor, and the result is a fascinating protagonist for this rich novel." —*Publishers Weekly*

"One of the most exciting books of 2015 . . . A fierce, provocative examination of childbirth and new motherhood." —*Buzzfeed*

"Astonishingly good." —Sarah Rachel Egelman, *Book Reporter*

"Anyone who's just had a baby absolutely needs to read this."

—Emily Gould, *Paper* magazine

BOOKS BY ELISA ALBERT

How This Night Is Different

The Book of Dahlia

Freud's Blind Spot (editor)

AFTER BIRTH

ELISA ALBERT

MARINER BOOKS
HOUGHTON MIFFLIN HARCOURT
Boston New York

First Mariner Books edition 2016

www.hmhco.com

Library of Congress Cataloging-in-Publication Data
Albert, Elisa, date.
After Birth / Elisa Albert.
pages cm
ISBN 978-0-544-27373-3 (hardback) ISBN 978-0-544-58291-0 (pbk)
1. Motherhood—Fiction. 2. Female friendship—Fiction. I. Title.
PS3601.L3344A69 2015
813'.6—dc23
2014006756
ISBN 978-0-544-27373-3

Book design by Greta D. Sibley

Printed in the United States of America
DOC 10 9 8 7 6 5 4 3 2 1

Parts of this book have appeared in a different form in *Tin House*.

For my husband

I have found out another funny thing, but I shan't tell it this time! It does not do to trust people too much.

—Charlotte Perkins Gilman, *The Yellow Wallpaper*

Why is it that when a woman tells a terrible story, no one, not even her own mother, believes her?

—Viva, *The Baby*

AFTER BIRTH

1

NOVEMBER

The buildings are amazing in this shitbox town.

Late eighteenth-century row houses. Dirt-basement Colonial wonders. High-ceilinged Victorians. Clapboards. Wood stoves, crappy plumbing, gracious proportions. Faded grandeur, semi-rot. Clawfoot bathtubs with old brass fixtures rusty as hell. Here and there the odd sparkling restoration. Someone's nouveau riche marble kitchen.

Here's my favorite: four-story brick, three windows wide, with a Historical Society Landmark plaque. Built in 1868. Elaborate molding painted many shades of green. My friends Crispin and Jerry spent the better part of ten years rehabbing it. They're on sabbatical this year in Rome, those bastards. They sublet to this amazing poet with a visiting gig at the college. Mina Morris. I'm a little obsessed with her, by which I mean a lot, which I guess is what obsessed means.

The parlor curtains are open and the lights are off.

I drove Crisp and Jer to the airport, and Crisp handed me an estate-sale mother-of-pearl cigarette case perfectly filled with nine meticulously rolled joints.

I teared up.

Medicine man, please don't go.

Listen. He lifted my chin and met my eyes in this avuncular way he has. *You've come a long way. You're going to be fine.* He said it slowly, like I might be very old, very stupid, or both.

I have five joints left.

The baby's first birthday approaches. Still, there are bad days. Today's not so bad. Today I have fulfilled two imperatives: one, the baby is napping; two, we are out of doors, a few blocks from home.

Anyway, Mina Morris. Crisp gave me her contact info because we're supposed to be landlord proxy, Paul and I, take care of anything that comes up with the house while they're gone.

Mina Morris. Quasi known as the bass player from the Misogynists. Girl band, Oregon, late eighties. Lots of better-known girl bands talk about having been influenced by them.

Cold this week, and dark so early. Late afternoon and the light is dead. So it begins: months of early darkness and cold. November again, back around to another. Last November a nightmare blur of newborn stitches tears antibiotics awake constipation tears wound tears awake awake awake limping tears screaming tears screaming shit piss puke tears. My weeks structured around a very occasional trip to the drive-through donut place near the mall, baby dozing in the back. Idling in the crappy old Jewish cemetery across the highway, heat cranked, reading names on crooked headstones, sipping an enormous, too-sweet latte, tapping at the disappointing glow of my device.

Faint whistle. There goes a train. To the city, probably. Four fifteen. Too late for the baby's nap now, too close to bedtime. But I've given up trying to control this shit. If you have an agenda, any needs or desires of your own (like, for example, to take a shower, take a dump, be somewhere at a given time, sit and think), you're screwed. The trick is to surrender completely, take your moments when you get them, don't dare want for more.

Mina Morris: poet, erstwhile rock star. Here, in Crisp and Jerry's house. Gives me an obscure little thrill, it does. I want to be friends.

A third-floor light goes on, and simultaneously the baby starts up with the whimpers. I take my cue. Keep the stroller moving, always moving, my reflexive animal sway. Respite over. Maneuver down the block toward the river, up Chestnut, and on home. Put some cheese on crackers and call it dinner.

Another day gone, okay, and I get it, I got it: I'm over. I no longer exist. This is why there's that ancient stipulation about the childless being ineligible for the study of religious mysticism. This is why there's all that talk about kid having as express train to enlightenment. You can meditate, you can medicate, you can take peyote in the desert at sunrise, you can self-immolate, or you can have a baby, and disappear.

I'm not interested in anything.

Ari. Babe.

Which might make sense if I was all consumed with thoughts of baby-food making and craft projects and sleep-training philosophies and bouncy-chair brands, but I really can't get all that excited about any of that shit either. So basically I have no idea what to do with myself, Paul.

Babe. Give it some time.

Fine, I mean, great, but how much time? He's one, Paul.

Exactly, babe, he's one.

You should just send me away someplace. You should just take me out back and shoot me.

Ari.

Utrecht, New York: the valiant but disgusting Bottomless Cup, the filthy antique shop with unpredictable hours, the burrito bar with blurry pane glass. Windowless Ozzy's, the diviest bar ever, embodiment of dive, hilarious exaggeration of dive: jaundiced, wispy-haired men in stonewashed denim smoking endless cigarettes and playing pool on a disintegrating table at eleven in the morning. The tiny cheesecake-burlesque joint run by kids (it's funny how you start calling them kids) who graduated a few years ago and are committed to local regeneration. They smoke weed and bake all day, act sort of put out when you come in wanting a slice of caramel toffee and some tea. Long-empty storefront, recently empty storefront, long-empty storefront.

Two hundred miles directly up the river on the east side, forty-five minutes past the sweet antiques, the second homes. A town, I guess you'd call it, a once-upon-a-time town, some blocks of cheap, amazing, mostly run-down houses crying out for restoration by the likes of us. We are happy to oblige them, the houses. We live like kings. When Paul got this job

I was six months pregnant and we thought: okay, yeah, go fuck yourself, Brooklyn! We spent like a hundred dollars on an amazing 1872 four-bedroom Italianate with a killer porch and congratulated ourselves on the excellent aesthetic of it all, no "good" school district for miles, low volume of hyper-ambitious creative aspirants, stoic wide planks groaning wisely underfoot.

Our accountant works out of the creaky Albany townhouse where Herman Melville spent part of his childhood. There's an okay coffee roaster, a tiny wine bar, a tinier used-book store, and a shitbox convenience store. And the food co-op two towns over where I work Fridays like a good little citizen. Sometimes I even wear the baby around in a sling.

The college in town is pretty much its own thing—rich kids who didn't get into fill-in-the-blank—and the town, or quasi town, has been in varying stages of rot for a while. Some faculty live in this handful of blocks, in these amazing, intermittently neglected houses sloping down toward the overgrown banks of the river; others live in head-shakingly unattractive suburbs spreading out like rays from the sun of the mall. A stubborn few actually commute from the city, refuse to be separated from that fucking city, not even for wildly affordable pocket doors and stained glass and exquisite molding and antique tile and anti-glamorous/glamorous social annihilation.

In the early nineteenth century, Utrecht was the center of shirt-cuff manufacturing. Big bustling factory supported the entire town until a succession of patents changed shirt-cuff manufacturing forever, mass production, outsourcing, what have you, and Utrecht withered like a corpse. A dump, to be sure, but still, a kind of particularly sweet Hudson Valley dump. A shirt-cuff bigwig founded the college in 1845, purportedly because his son didn't get into Harvard.

Remnants of the shirt-cuff era abound. A leathery, delightful old girl band called the Cuffs. The empty shell of the mill downriver. Once in a while there's a spirited movement to turn it into some sort of performance space, a DIY community center they want to call "the Downriver," but local bureaucrats crush that regenerative shit time and again, dashing the hopes of our sweet, stoned cheesecake artistes.

Few blocks in any direction are desperate slums, and on Sundays you can't so much as buy a newspaper within a mile. But there's a tiny, unpretentious farmers' market in the courtyard of a vacant mini-mall on the edge of town, and a chain pharmacy just opened a ways down Main Street, in a long-empty storefront that was for a hundred years a jewelry store. BARLOW AND SONS, EST. 1893: you can still see remnants of the old gold lettering. The chain pharmacy didn't even bother to fully renovate. Just slapped a fluorescent sign over the door and drywalled the interior.

First official Mina Morris sighting. My heart did an Olympic dive. Bulk section at the co-op. Unwashed hair in loose knot, filling a bag with organic honey caramels. I watched her unwrap one and pop it into her mouth. Total insouciance. Gorgeous creature. And! She is way pregnant. Hard-not-to-stare pregnant.

I wrote to her months ago, *hey* and *if you need anything* and *welcome to our shithole* and *please don't hesitate,* blah blah, and an elaborately casual offer of *tea or something anytime.* Spent like half an hour trying to make it sound casual, cut down from the volumes in my head. Embarrassing. I have zero friends here.

She responded immediately, in full: *cool thanks.*

Meanwhile I devoured her book. Weird beautiful bewildered little prose poems about the summer of 1990, mostly, just after the Misogynists broke up. Roaming Europe, shooting up, regularly letting a disgusting man named Ivan pay to fuck her up the ass, pining for some nameless bastard with a wife in Paris. Then her family brings her home and puts her away. Electroshock. And the best part is how she just kind of leaves you there, wondering if she'll make it out all right. Which, I mean, to whatever degree, it appears she has, but *Jesus.* Makes my own fucked-up shit seem downright housewifely.

I held the book close when I finished, actually embraced the thing. Had the inclination to rip out and ingest a page, for the same reason you might get a tattoo, so it'll stay a part of you, edify you forever.

Paul has no idea who the Misogynists are. That's Paul in a nutshell. He can tell you what foods gave Whitman gas, though.

They sound familiar, I think, he said in the spring, when the department announced Mina was coming. It was a nice night, almost warm, the worst of winter receding.

Paul's colleague Cat was over. She sat bolt upright, set her wineglass on the floor.

Nuh-uh, don't even. You don't know the Misogynists? "Eat Me While I Decide"? "Can't Stop Wanting"? "Who the Fuck Are You"?

Paul shrugged. Cat is always really appalled when other

people don't share her precise cultural context. Crispin once described it that way. He meant it as an insult, I'm pretty sure, but it's one of the things I actually like about Cat: the way she wants us all on the same page, the way she seems sort of angry, betrayed, when it appears that we are not all on the same page.

Wait, she said, tapping at her device. *Wait, wait. Here.*

Promptly we hooked up the speakers and were joyously assaulted by a Misogynists number. *Na na na hey hey hey suck my clit and we'll call it a day.*

Subtle, Paul said.

I saw them at the Paradise in 1989, Cat said. *Right before they broke up and Kelly died.*

Cat needs you to know that she's seen things, knows people, has been in the right place at the right time even if she's currently in the wrong place all the time.

Paul went up to bed. *Have fun, ladies.*

If we get drunk or high enough, we can usually rally some sort of good time, Cat and I, at least a little sliver of fun, but sometimes we try and try and only end up morose and drunk/high, side by side. Then we don't hang out for a while and it's like we've never hung out next time we hang out and I get inexplicably mad at Paul, like how could you do this to me, make me this desperate isolated hausfrau scrounging for simpaticos in this backwater shitbox?

The first girl I ever loved was Nora Pulaski. Adorable athletic little doe-eyed cutie. First day of kindergarten she sits down next to me with all the assurance of her almost six years, gives me this knowing look, and informs me that we are going to be best friends.

Thrilling. She chose me. I don't think I even wondered why.

We played with Barbies and rearranged the furniture in the elaborate dollhouse my father bought me the first time my mother was sick. Moved through all the levels of cat's cradle, practiced cartwheels in the unfurnished living room of Nora's rental on East Fifty-Seventh, coauthored a pamphlet of appreciation for the third-grade boy we both loved, a skinny, freckled redhead. Strange choice, that kid, but wow did we love him. We drew his name in bubble letters so many times.

Nora was confident, at home in herself. Her mom was calm and made us muffins. Once I heard Nora call her Mommy, which surprised me, because mine was strictly Janice. "Mommy" sounded so fond, so assumptive. I would no sooner call mine Mommy than throw myself into the arms of a stranger on the subway.

Around fifth grade we had this game in which I was Hugo and Nora was Nancy. Hugo would return home from a day of work "horny," and Nancy would be waiting for him on the bed, and we would grind for a while.

One time Nora's mom stretched out on the couch with us while we watched TV. She smoothed my hair, murmured *how's your mom, sweetheart,* and I froze. Couldn't speak for fear I'd lose it (lose what?), shake out some highly embarrassing primal wail.

By middle school, when my mom was dead, Nora got new friends. Smart girls. Confident girls. Girls with good mothers. Girls who were going to work from within the system and kick ass in college. She still said hi to me, wasn't ever mean or anything, but we weren't friends anymore.

• • •

I love fucking Paul.

Sometimes it's like being on a floating dock in a breeze; sometimes it's like saying goodbye aboard a failing airplane. Tonight it's like a firm handshake to seal a deal.

I was with a series of angry fuckers up til Paul, real flip-you-over-try-to-hurt-you types, not a lot of eye contact. Thought I was having fun.

Such sweet beginnings we had, me and Paul. The delicious, clandestine smell of him on my sheets. Nothing intellectual about it, just wanted to bury my face in his skin, breathe him. Gave me the shivers. He's the kind of guy who'll fuck you nice and slow. But sweet beginnings are not the challenge, now, are they.

We kept it secret for almost a year. There was the whiff of scandal: he an associate professor and I a grad student fifteen years his junior. Apparently they still frown on that sort of thing. Ridiculous, besides which he already had tenure. But there was also the issue of his long-term, long-distance girlfriend, a theory-of-theory-of-theory type stuck on the tenure track in some godforsaken corner of Indiana.

Commitment-phobe, my bitchiest friend, Subeena, warned me. *He's* how *old? They've been together* how *long?*

We have an agreement, Paul told me. *We live our own lives.*

But when he finally broke it off with her, she was livid, absolutely devastated, and he could not wrap his head around why.

We had an agreement, he pointed out.

I gave up having children for you, she said, and wept.

You said you didn't even want *kids,* he told her.

Don't you love those women who ignore every imperative of time and biology then act all super-duper tragic at forty? Come on, now.

Tonight we huddle naked under the down, laughing about funny things the baby's doing lately. He is cool, we agree. Cracks us up. Of this much we are certain: he is a sweet boy, a funny sunny love of a boy. He has this way of smiling at us, this sly little grin. We adore him. Oh, do we ever. We're happy. We're blessed. We are we are we are we are. Knock wood, spit three times, wave garlic, throw a pinch of salt, whatever you got.

You keep saying how happy you are, my favorite professor, Marianne, said over coffee last year when we were supposed to be talking about my dissertation. *You keep saying that. You just told me four times how happy you are. I am happy for you that you are so happy.*

A minute or hour later I'm awake from a dream, sweaty: my cousin Jason brought a prostitute to my father's old family house in the Berkshires and woke everybody up with their humping. I hadn't seen everyone in a long time, all together. My grandparents, Aunt Ellen, cousins Jason and Erica. Even my mother was there, spectral but healthy. The prostitute was Mina Morris twenty years ago: stringy hair, dark lipstick, addicted, wild-eyed, half-crazy.

I was sleeping! my mother screamed at no one in particular, stomping around in a thin pink nightgown. I could see her heavy breasts in shadow. *You woke me up, you inconsiderate little shits!* She used to call me that, like a term of endearment.

Shut the fuck up, bitch, Mina Morris told her coldly, and my mother was shocked silent for once.

My father sold that house in the Berkshires years ago. Aunt Ellen has barely spoken to me since I married Paul, though she did send a handwritten letter, lot of *disappointed* and *history* and *our people* and *suffered enough,* which I pretended to disregard but later tore up in a rage and flushed down the toilet. Cousin Jason is highly religious, lives in Arizona, works "for the government," and wants further proof that President Obama was born in the United States. In his profile picture he is wearing a novelty Israeli Army T-shirt, stone-cold serious. Erica lives in the city working wholeheartedly the kind of fashion rag you read if your highest aspiration is Best Dressed at cosmetology school. We used to go out for drinks when we were in our twenties. She sent a very fancy onesie for the baby.

I'm awake, is the point, drenched, and there's this thumping, now scratching, now thumping again coming from inside the ceiling.

Crap, Paul whispers.

Mouse?

Bigger. Squirrel. I don't know. Raccoon. Fuck.

Paul is your basically stoic, healthy, strictly uncomplaining non-Jew. He's hard to ruffle. He's never had a cold. Once, just one time, I got him mad enough to yell at me, and was perversely thrilled he had it in him. The sex afterward was epic.

I thought a trapped animal in the wall of a house was only, like, a literary device.

He slides a hand between my thighs, mutters something about calling Will in the morning, and goes back to sleep.

Takes me a while longer, though, because it's pretty noisy inside the ceiling or the wall or whatever, and I'm not exactly eager to see my mother again.

This time I dream it's summertime and sunshine streams from between my thighs, radiating softly around my hips. I am very, very pregnant and very, very happy. Sunshine within, sunshine without, gold and warm. But something is wrong with our house. Will comes over. He brings me a sloppy fistful of wildflowers, lays them on the counter. He gestures at my glowing middle, averts his eyes.

Amazing thing you're doing there, Ari. Totally amazing.

I don't know where Paul is. Will heads to the basement to examine the furnace, which I realize is too hot, intensifying the sunshine unbearably. There is burning through the whole house, burning in every room, everything melting together: happy and yellow, smelling of beeswax and cum.

Some hours or minutes pass this way, then there's Mr. Baby, howling at the pale, icy dawn.

Raccoon! says Will when he and Paul come clomping down from the attic. *Pretty sure. There's an opening near the baseboard under the window.*

The baby toddles over, hides behind my legs. He's an awesome baby, a swell little guy. Still a baby, though, of which even the best are oppressive fascist bastard dictator narcissists.

So what do we do?

Paul's slumped at the counter, head in hands. *Move.*

Will shrugs. *Traps. The good kind. Weather turns, you know, they find ways in. Cold out there. Can't blame them.*

Will's parents were professors at the college. He ran from them, from here, became a carpenter. Worked on boats on the South Shore of Boston for a long time, drank and drank and drank and drank. Found his way to AA and Thich Nhat

Hanh and mindful awareness. Came back here when the professors died. To *face it,* he told me once. Our eyes met and we understood each other. We have to be careful with eye contact, me and Will. We avoid it as best we can, good soldiers, everything on the up-and-up.

So he fixed up their old house, three down from ours. Knows how to do all sorts of useful things. Welds in the garage, helps us figure out the rudiments of boilers, roofing, basement finishing, painting, electricity, stays for dinner, eats my slow-cooker hippie food, says *whatever* and *no biggie* and *glad to help.* Fifty-one, tall, floppy hair, runner's body, lined face, piercing gray eyes, strong hands, cool dirty sneakers. I regularly imagine fucking him for a long afternoon in a highway motel where the bleach doesn't quite cover the smell.

The baby puts his hand near the oven, admonishes himself with an approximation of "hot!" and looks for approval. I offer it up: *yes that's right good boy who's a good boy you are oh you're such a good good boy!*

Who can say I'm not a good mother? Who can say I don't read the subject headings in the books? The How to Care for Your Child if There Is Absolutely No One with Any Primal Knowledge Around to Guide You guides. What to Expect When There Is No Received Wisdom Whatsoever. I keep them in an out-of-the-way drawer, like porn.

Can't we just, like, seal off wherever it got in? Paul has his arcane PhD, his prestigious appointment, but no idea how to strip paint or tighten a pipe fitting or deal with a rodent.

You don't want him in there. He'll die in there. You guys have peanut butter?

Paul brightens, reaches an arm around my waist, or what

used to be my waist. *Yeah, we can rustle up some peanut butter. Ari, stay out of the traps, will you?* The joke being that I'm not as lithe as before I fabricated and surgically evacuated a new human being, fuck you very much. I like to go at the peanut butter with a spoon. Before he's finished the sentence he understands that he has made a mistake, and his face turns sorry.

Prick.

Yes, clearly I am not as lithe as before I fabricated and surgically evacuated a new human being. At any opportunity my stepmother will still give me the Scan, let's call it, that classic down-up as common to the female of the species as is the vagina—and offer a specious *don't worry, sweetie, you'll get back to normal soon.* Bitch, I mean, come on: do you think I don't know I'm wearing enormous pants?

The baby's first birthday.

Surgery day, I point out, because I have trouble calling it birth. Anniversary of the great failure.

Ari. Don't.

Can't handle a party, none of that circus shit. Baby doesn't know the difference. We give him his first taste of ice cream after dinner, sing the song, blow out a candle on his behalf, clap, kiss. We forget to take pictures. The joyful chocolate-faced baby, lone candle, flurry of my desperate attempts at good cheer.

Will comes over with a bottle of good scotch.

We made it, babe, Paul says, toasting. Who exactly does he imagine as having made it? And to where? All we've done is get used to it.

Clink. I'm surrounded by sweet males. There is that.

I was on happy pills in college, but they messed with my memory and made me fat, so I ditched them. Regularly Paul wonders whether it might be time to check back in with some meds again, maybe "talk to someone." I bristle. I want to feel things about things. Sad that I don't have a mother and that the one I had was a total bitch. Mad at my ball-sack OB for gutting me like a fucking fish for no good reason. Surprised and frustrated that even the best man on earth turns out not to cure loneliness. Bored to tears by my own in-depth examination of a subject I once adored. Worn down by the drudgery and isolation of caring for a tiny child.

He was born on a Tuesday after a long day of labor, but I did not "give" birth to him. He was not "given" birth. The great privilege.

Instead, the knife.

He was "late," they said. Late, late for a purely invented date. So he got evicted, and everything went south, and me too complacent to challenge, too stupid to question. Why so stupid? Why so complacent?

They cut me in half, pulled the baby from my numb, gaping, cauterized center. Merciless hospital lights, curtain in front of my face. Effective disembodiment. Smell of burning flesh. Sewn back up again by a team of people I didn't know, none of whom bothered to look me in the eye, not even one of them, not even once. Severed from hip to hip, iced, brutalized, catheterized, tethered to a bed, the tiny bird's heartfelt shrieks as they carted him off somewhere hell itself.

I could barely move for days, let alone entertain rational thoughts about the soft, small bundle of bottomless need they placed in my arms later, when I awoke in the wrong kind of pain entirely.

We were sent home after the requisite, terrible bowel movement. In the shocking days that followed I saw the requisite awfulness: the baby harmed, the baby hurt, the baby suffering, the baby hurled to the ground, the baby's head crushed against the wall, destroyed. Ongoing fever dream. In the grip of a kind of black magic for which I was entirely unprepared. Woke in a sweat from intermittent sleep to find him still—oh thank God, thank God—breathing.

He's breathing okay he's breathing okay he's breathing okay. Okay. Okay. Okay. I wandered too near the white-hot root of things. Flummoxed. Wedded now to a possibility of loss so extreme I could barely breathe myself.

The baby books said nothing about this. Days became nights became days became nights. The baby books said nothing! I held him tight, held him close. Would not let go. The harm that could come to him! The consequence of just one misstep! Unthinkable. Unbearable. What now? What next?

I'll take him, babe, Paul would say. *Give him to me. Try and get some rest.*

My infected incision oozed, tight phony grin of a sadistic monster. The necessary course of antibiotics.

I had died, was dead, only a ghost, not fully gone. Watch him breathe: is he breathing? Hold him close. Move slow, wrap yourself around him. Easy, easy. Don't hurt him. Careful. Is he alive? The world so hideously perilous and the baby a raw egg, only of its kind.

Paul's mother in Ohio called every third day.

How are you doing? I don't want to bother you.

How am I. I don't really know. I don't know how people are supposed to do this. I don't know how to do this.

New babies are a lot of work!

I need help, I told her. *I can't do this.* My voice was low. She's good people. Retired secretary, grew up on a farm, hardcore quilter, loves her some sitcoms.

Don't be silly. Of course you can.

A woman who's known her whole life how to grow fruits and vegetables, how to can them in the fall, how to sew a dress from a pattern, how to knit a sweater, how to care for the sick. A master of the womanly arts. She was my best bet. Surely she would hightail it over here immediately, show me how. Demonstrate so I might learn.

This child's mother needs to come and get him now, I said. *Someone needs to come and get him. Everything hurts. I'm so tired.*

How's the weather out there, she wondered. *I'd better let you go.*

A year later, now—happy birthday, moppet—and still I'm working hard to stand up straight, wearing pajamas all the time, avoiding the scar at all costs, suffering these surprise dunks in the rage tank. And occasionally people I barely know cheerfully wonder: *are you going to have another?*

We're not to rest until the raccoon is gone. The ways in which he might destroy our lives and house are many: chew through electrical wiring, piss and shit all over the insides of walls, lead others in. He could die and rot. He could have rabies. He could terrorize the baby. He could have babies with rabies who will terrorize the baby.

Will brings over two enormous wire cage traps and sets them up on opposite walls of the attic. While he's at it he replaces our screens with storms, eliminates the draft. He stays for couscous and mushrooms, makes the baby giggle, tells us a story about a critter problem in a house a mile downriver. Something about a family of animals in a sealed-off wall, months later a HAZMAT crew.

But nah, don't worry, he says. He clamps Paul on the shoulder—*'night, bro*—offers me a sweet, somber salute from the steps. Will's a smart guy. Not smart as in advanced degree; smart as in knows how to be.

Another Mina sighting this morning on the way to day care. She was lumbering up Crisp and Jer's front steps, keys in hand. Couldn't bring myself to approach her, so instinctively I labeled her a total bitch. That's my automatic thing with women. They're guilty until proven innocent.

Her pregnancy is surprising. She's well north of forty, and the Internet offers nothing on the subject of a man. The Internet offers precious little in general, which of course is the only way you can remotely respect anyone: when you don't find too much bullshit self-generated virtual PR.

Four days a week, so that I might "work on my dissertation," I hand the baby over to Nasreen at day care. He wails *maaaa-maaaaa* all desperate, reaches for me with little clutching hands. Pure awful. Full-body apocalypse.

He puts on good show for you, Nasreen says. She is Pakistani and has seven children, the oldest four of whom still live in Pakistan with her sister. *He is fine. You leave, he is fine.*

She shoos me out, rolls her eyes. These stupid mothers.

It's like my heart's being ripped out of my chest, and I'm supposed to walk away like no biggie. I hide on the other side of the door for two minutes until his wailing abates, then slink off like a criminal. Nausea, regret, darkness, light, relief, freedom, joy, ache, guilt, confusion, elation: all in equal measure, like your first orgasm.

When I am with my precious peanut, I itch to hand him over; when I hand him over, I itch to take him back and never let him go.

My dissertation is not happening.

Mostly I read celebrity blind items, stalk successful acquaintances, check the prep time for adzuki beans, look at headlines, make the bed, scroll through surreal early pictures of the baby, tiny terrifying thing. Generally waste time as though there are endless tomorrows.

Here's Mina in a band photo circa 1988, wearing thrift shop clothes. Not fashionable thrift shop clothes, mind you—filthy, ill-fitting thrift shop clothes. Hair's matted. They're under a fire escape in an alley, brick walls close around. Kelly is squatting, cold. Stefani stands over her, arms crossed. Mina leans back against a wall, indifferent and apart, glancing over at the camera like it's an unattractive stranger requesting a hand job. She would have been around twenty, then. The youngest. Cheeks like pillows.

A dimly lit video of a reading in a bar, her voice gravelly and worn. I love how she isn't all toothy, doesn't exclaim and prance and coo and spin that *do you like me gosh I really hope you do because I am very likable* shit, which seems in a lot of women to get only higher-pitched as years unfold. She doesn't care whether or not you like her. She's wearing an ugly T-shirt, her hair is dirty. She's not worried about whether you think she's pretty. She's reading a poem. A good one. You can get on board or you can go fuck yourself.

And here: vaguely embarrassed in an interview with a preening blogger.

And here: forty-nine seconds of grainy footage from a club in Eugene decades ago. The sound is bad. She's in the back, barely visible, playing her bass sideways, eyes closed. Like she's trying to forget about the audience. Like the audience is a mild inconvenience. Stefani apes for the camera from behind the drums, and Kelly screams at the mic, attacking her guitar, disturbed and desperate. They never made it past those clubs, never moved beyond those small shows. But a lot of people who saw them felt transformed. Bootlegs circulated. One band formed in homage got pretty big.

Here: on a gray day in Maine, the author photo. Hair blowing across her unsmiling face. Muddy boots.

Okay. Enough. Something else. Recent study shows national 12 percent increase in male-fetus miscarriages during the month following the World Trade Center attacks. Scientists discover a type of stress hormone secreted in the brain while subjects surf the Internet. Some bitch on a Southwest flight smacks her baby for crying; heroic flight attendant immediately takes custody of baby. Woman updates her status with a brief, misspelled plea for forgiveness before driving herself and her four children off a bridge. The bees continue to disappear. At least 120 dead bodies lie frozen all along the peak ascent of Mount Everest. Woman with fake smile tells odorous tale of egg donors, gestational surrogates; accompanying photo showcases twin "miracles" trussed like holiday turkeys.

I stare at the screen this way for a while. Delicious, terrible inaction. And soon enough it's time to get the baby from Nasreen's.

Just want to sit here instead, in the fading light from the big window, in the sonic embrace of the speakers. Nasreen takes good care of him. Nasreen knows how. It's good for him there. Better, even, probably.

There's a curt email from Marianne about the dissertation. How's the thinking coming? Any commitment to any particular focus?

Simultaneously I yearn for the sweet munchkin—what have you accomplished today you terrible wench why aren't you with your munchkin don't you know your munchkin needs you get off your fat ass and GO—and continue to sit here, precious peanut in someone else's arms.

Does Marianne actually think I'm working on my dissertation? Does she think I give a flying fuck about my dissertation? It's all I can do to bathe occasionally, keep the house reasonably tidy, feed us, launder, get some sleep. Literally: all I can do.

Like I give a shit about my dissertation.

Your creative energy is being utilized elsewhere, a kindly massage therapist informed me as pregnancy wore on. Then she hugged me, did some acupressure, some Reiki.

So the dissertation thing is pretty much a lie. But you need an identity, some interest and occupation outside of having a kid, you just do. Otherwise the kid has to be your sole interest and occupation, and we all know how *that* works out for everyone.

Our house was probably owned by some terrible textile executive at the end of the empire. I imagine him depressed, insolvent on the cusp of the Great Depression. He shoots himself in the head, a letter on the desk for his wife (the second; the first died in childbirth) and one for his mistress (a scullery maid, perhaps?). The den must have been showered with blood and brain, the children screaming, the house cursed, any lurking unhappiness here simply the result. Places hold things; you have to be an asshole not to acknowledge that. Bodies, houses, earth: feelings, energy, spirit. Deny them if you must, they don't care. Call them what you will.

It's got built-in bookshelves and delicate gold-leaf floral wallpaper so old and faded it's gorgeous once again. Before we moved in it had sat empty for three years after the very last of the maiden aunts died at ninety-seven in a nursing home. It's got original windows and deep mahogany pocket shutters. The kitchen must have been state-of-the-art, a real point of pride back in 1920, when the future looked bright. The fledgling brood so full of promise, the young couple expecting their first child, laughing together, all life's horrors still to come.

At the baby's sixth-month checkup a pediatric nurse asked a series of robotic questions—*have you thought about harming yourself or the baby are there guns in your house has the baby's father ever threatened you are you depressed in any way*. I didn't say I imagined shooting myself twenty times a day. I didn't say I took strange, enormous comfort in these visions. I said *there are no guns in our house*. I said *um I guess a little depressed sort of yeah*. She made a decisive mark on my chart, sent in the doctor. Nice guy, vegetarian, makes intelligent small talk while he does his exam, doesn't try to sell us on all the vaccines all at once. Told me to get as much help around the house as we could afford. Told me to find a group.

No idea how to find help, but okay, a group. Drove up to Albany a couple times.

Lots of the women in the group had surgeries, too. They either didn't speak of it or they spoke of it as perfectly normal, which, I guess, hey, it is. They spoke of Zumba, stroller recalls, nursery schools, new hibachi place out by the mall.

Who knew motherhood could be a mostly material experience? We'd sit in Starbucks rooting around in pastel-camouflage diaper bags for chew toys and muslin wraps while women without babies gave us endless dirty looks. Me and this one silent, dark-eyed woman the only ones breastfeeding; the others busy with chemistry experiments: powders, cold packs, bottles.

The poor babies were beside the point, like half-forgotten elderly consigned to our care. The girl babies looked like drag queens: ruffles and bows, a flower-and-rhinestone headpiece. One thusly adorned kept giving me a hilariously cranky look like *can you believe this shit?* She was cool. I winked at her like *sorry, honey, I know, but it's not forever, I swear.*

One of the moms had elective surgery because she just *didn't really like the whole unknown part* and *really wanted him to get here in time for his first Christmas.* Another, a marathoner with the calves to prove it, called childbirth *unnecessary.*

Drag queen's mom said *I'm not that great with pain and Dave was just grossed out by the whole thing, so we decided just get it over with.* She went on to tell about how she was administered a muscle relaxant by mistake mid-surgery. When she realized she couldn't breathe, there was madness trying to get the baby out before *it* got dosed and she very nearly died on the table and the kid was in the NICU for a week but *we got a free room out of it and they were suuuuper nice 'cause Dave said they were worried we might sue.*

One was sent home two days post-surgery only to pass out cold in the bathroom in septic shock; they had to leave the newborn with a neighbor they barely knew while they got her to the emergency room with a nicked bowel.

One's due date had been completely miscalculated, so when they dove in, the baby was underweight, couldn't breathe on its own, spent three weeks in the NICU.

Yet another, totally affectless, told of a constant numb tingling all up and down her right leg from the spinal and said *there's nothing I can do about it at this point, so why do we keep having to* talk *about it?*

I got lucky, someone said. *They only had to use the vacuum extractor.*

Yeah, see, that's why I'm glad we just went with the C, said the drag queen's mom. *I hear those things really mess up your vag.*

I asked them if they feel good about their birth experience. They examined me crossly. One giggled.

Birth Experience, she said. *Sounds like a ride at Disney.*

Feel good about it like, you mean, glad it's over?

Feel good about it like, enjoyed it?

A few months later I tried another group, thirty minutes in a different direction.

I was to let Walker watch his father and me on the toilet, talk about the toilet, encourage familiarity with the toilet. I was to make sure he ate at least a cup of vegetables every day. There was the possibility of someday locking him in his room at night if he resisted sleep. There was pediatric dentistry to consider. There was early intervention for absolutely anything.

Imagine: I had dared to imagine that we would talk to one another, that the boring specifics of child rearing would be *incidental.*

I mean, let's pause to acknowledge that it's possible to be a good mother while doing other things. You know: multitasking. Scouting the horizon for tigers. Gathering herbs. Stirring the pot. Reading a fucking newspaper.

Even the laid-back granola DIY homestead types were anal shrews about their laid-back-ness. Over email a fight broke out. A sippy-cup brand disagreement devolved into a fight in which one predicted a life of crime for the other's child. Tireless. Just take care of business, ladies. Don't make a fucking hobby out of it. Feed the kid, bathe the kid, help the kid to sleep, hug and kiss and smile and hug and kiss some more until they're too old for that; then just try to model the best behavior you possibly can for the rest of your life, and do it again tomorrow; it's not fucking science. Find some other things to think about.

I'm not going to pretend my kid is special, like other kids who starve and freeze and get raped and beaten and have to work in factories and get cancer from the fumes, too bad, so sad, but my kid is going to be warm and organic and toxin-free and safe and have everything he wants when he wants it and go to a good college and all is right with the world! Fuck that myopic bullshit. He's going to suffer. He's going to get mauled by some force I can't pretend I can predict. We all live in the same fucked-up world.

Then there were stories about how this or that one just couldn't breastfeed, her sister gave it up after two months or six months or a year because it hurt or she just didn't have any milk or come on, enough was enough, or hey, isn't there all sorts of unfair pressure on women to nurse and shouldn't it be, like, a choice? Yes, ladies. Congratulations: you have choices.

A chore, trying to talk to these women. You saw them calcifying. You saw them race to this endpoint, then come to a stop and calcify, never to move again.

I practiced my blank stare. How noble of you to plug your kid with some processed milk-derivative shit marketed by the same people who brought the world Oreos, how very feminist of you, yes, every woman makes her choices, absolutely, what glorious freedom we enjoy. Way to stick it to the man. How empowered you are, subverting a basic function of your body. May I shake your hand? You show that body of yours who's boss! You get on with your bad self. What shipshape shiny master's tools you've got there. How's the dismantling of the master's house working out?

A Friday. My shift at the co-op. Box and bag groceries, sort recycled plastic, align merchandise on the shelves. (This last is called, amusingly, "fronting.")

Naomi is my boss. Twenty-three, dropped out of SUNY sophomore year, lives in an abandoned nineteenth-century savings bank in Troy with three art students and fourteen stray cats. They throw massive dance parties that start at midnight on the last Friday of every month.

She is forever handing out flyers.

Coming Friday? She's adorable, and makes me feel old.

Gonna try, I always lie.

• • •

My second friend was Jenny Jacobson, of the alliterative name and showbiz aspirations. She had an agent, went on constant auditions for commercials, eventually booked an ad for cereal, real big deal. She was a powerful force in the sixth grade, respected and feared in equal measure. Everything turned to shit for her by eighth grade (bulimia, Bellevue), but she was still in her prime when I knew her.

Jenny's parents were getting a divorce. She had been prepped for the apocalypse with books about little girls whose parents were getting divorced, and with her very own shrink, Henri. They lived in a glass-and-steel penthouse on lower Park Avenue, and her father had this interesting way of staring at me but then looking away when I looked at him. I could actually *feel* his eyes on my little pubescent ass. And I didn't not enjoy it, either.

Henri says parents sometimes have to go separate ways in order to do the things they need to do to be happy and successful, and when my mom and dad are both doing the things they need to do separately all three of us are going to be much, much happier, so really it's a good thing and we're celebrating and I'm really glad they're getting divorced because when all three of us are happier it will be even better than if we all stayed together and weren't as happy or as successful. So we're having a divorce party and everything.

I almost liked being with her, I disliked her so much. It had an addictive flavor, hating her. One of those bossy little bitches who find a way to twist things so that she's always a winner, always triumphant, always in charge. Never screwed, never sad, never sorry, never at the mercy of others. One of those self-aggrandizing little bitches who refuse themselves any admission of weakness. Always play-acting that idiotic control. Jenny with her absurd mop of kinky orange curls, her freckles. The kind of girl who was going to spend her life demanding to be taken seriously. And no one takes those girls seriously.

She didn't scare me one little bit, and boy did that scare *her.*

She did this thing about my mother with huge watery eyes, being So Very Sorry for me, to imply that my mother was very close to dying—which she was, it was true—and that therefore I was a pitiful wretch.

It must be so very difficult for you that your mom is so very ill, she'd say reproachfully. The know-it-all tone, the superiority (her parents were just getting *divorced,* which was actually *great* news), the hierarchy of pain in which I was the winner, and so really the loser. She made me insane. I couldn't get enough of her.

Yeah, I guess, I said, incapable of spin. (We have lots of delicious Popsicles in our freezer 'cause she gets these huge mouth sores from the chemo, it's great!) The lights in our house were always dim. My mother spent months dying. Weeks and weeks tiptoeing up to the very, very, very end. It seemed that it could be any day for an enormous number of days.

How traaaaagic. Jenny gazed out her bedroom windows at the tops of other buildings. *What terrible circumstances. Such a difficult thing for a young girl.*

She's gonna be fine, I said, and almost had to laugh. She was not going to be fine. She was not going to be alive very much longer. She could be dead right then and I wouldn't know it until I went home. But something about those self-aggrandizing bitches makes it impossible for *you* to be weak, and so you wind up sorta *becoming* one of them, at least temporarily, to deal with them, which is so goddamn sad. It's a trap. You must avoid those bitches at all costs.

I don't think so, Jenny said. *And she's only in her forties! And with such a young daughter! So, so sad.* She looked like she was trying to make herself cry, like it was some kind of acting exercise. She reached out to pat my shoulder, and what did I do? Why, I punched her in the face. With closed fist. So satisfying. I can just about feel the shameful, electric pleasure of it reverberating up my arm even now.

Faculty party at Cameron and Betsy's tonight. An opportunity to put on decent clothes, something I don't have to yank down or up for boob access. Maybe a piece of jewelry, maybe go totally nuts, dab something shiny on the lips. Feels downright like Halloween.

Well, well, Cam bellows as we make our way up their stoop, three blocks away in a cold drizzle, the baby asleep under the care of a student babysitter. I pray she's not as stupid as she dresses, this babysitter. With her obnoxious ringtones and hot-pink sweats, COME HERE OFTEN printed across the ass. I pray she'll keep righteous watch.

Cam means well and wants to chill but doesn't know how and so channels all this crap energy into an aggressive sense of humor, like a mean older brother. Psychology department, I think. I try to ignore the details. He's a friend of Paul's, which because they're dudes seems to imply uncomplicated amiability from a remarkable distance, occasional scotch.

Betsy's chipper, constantly compensating for Cam. They have this whole act, these roles they play in their own little mutually agreed upon lifelong theatrical production. I fear that this is what long-term relationships are all about, at base: full-time role-playing, memorized and inhabited. They're always guzzling coffee, these two, as though trying to fortify themselves for another curtain.

Looks like Paul and Ari made it!

Looks that way, Bets. Looks that way.

Welcome! Come in, come in! How are you guys? What's up? Welcome! I like Betsy, really I do, but she is jittery as fuck, and she says everything twice.

They don't have kids, and they're closer to fifty than forty, some years past the point when they might have had kids but chose, or were chosen, not to.

Fairly badass on the one hand *not* to do this main thing we're forever exhorted to do, say *no thanks,* decline to buy an embryo from some God complex in a lab coat, decline to hire a hooker to cook it up. But the too-late-ness, on the other hand, the vanished possibility. The empty space. A lot to live with. A lot to live with either way, actually. Good title for a memoir! Fuck my dissertation. Life: It's a Lot to Live With.

Couple dozen people standing around. There's the French-theory bitch in Kabuki makeup, the sad divorced English department dude and his townie girlfriend. Art department stoner, hot sociopathic sculptor-in-band, insanely tense history couple, Cat. Jewish studies guy who's been extra special sweet to me since he found out about Grandma surviving the last Big Euro Jew Purge.

And oh, oh, oh: Mina.

Here she is, in the flesh. Leaning on the newel post talking to condescending poli-sci guy and his dead-eyed wife.

Go get her, tiger, Paul whispers.

Cam hands him a tumbler and turns to me.

Nothing for you, Ari? Still doing that whole—he waves a hand in the direction of my chest like he's trying to shake off something sticky—*baby . . . thing?*

It's not very hard to take Cam down: just flirt a little and he crumples instantly.

A demure smile, slide the shoulders down, tits out, reach calmly for a glass of wine, tall and proud, let the lips melt into repose, hold his gaze. Hold it . . . hold it . . . until he turns red and looks away and starts to perspire. And, done. Offer up the glass for a *clink* and walk away nice and slow.

I've always had a hard time differentiating between people who hate me and people who want to fuck me. Usually because, I finally realized, there's often a great deal of overlap.

I move toward the familiar disappointment of Cat, who's on the fringe of the Mina conversation. She takes me in (down, up) with that mysterious mixture of approval and disapproval, envy and superiority.

Hey, she says in her tight way. Cat was hired last year having only just barely lost out on a plum job in Seattle. We immediately became friends, and about five minutes later realized we didn't really like each other all that much. But you pretty much take what you can get around here.

Hey. I give her an awkward hug.

Mina looks more or less the same as in pictures, but older, realer, breathing. Very pregnant.

Condescending poli-sci guy is talking about a political candidate.

It's just so fucking predictable.

People nod.

I hide my face behind my wineglass. Talking politics is so

stupid. You either agree or you don't; either way you're no closer to a human exchange.

Mina's gone crinkly around the mouth and eyes. Amazing laugh lines. Still those full cheeks. Hair half-silver, maybe three-quarters. Soft, ragged old man jeans, none of the Lycra butt-crack prefaded grotesquerie. Ancient brown boots. Asymmetrical navy poncho in a low-key cotton/cashmere blend—unmistakably quality but appropriately pilled and loved. It'd look prissy new, and that right there's the thing most women don't understand about style: clothing must be worn, lived in, assimilated into uniform. Otherwise it's mere costume.

Six feet tall, I'd guess. Tattoos all up both arms, nose ring. Careworn. Hair in her eyes. Messy, artless, doesn't give a shit. Not like *trying to look like* she doesn't give a shit, actually does not give a shit. Probably the only comfortable woman in the room.

I wore my dumb punishing pointy boots from way, way back when they were in style. Cat's hair is dyed and shellacked a deep, awful magenta; Betsy's panty lines have panty lines. In the kitchen the French-theory bitch with the Kabuki face teeters on idiotic spike-heel contraptions resembling staplers. Someone should offer her bunions a glass of wine.

Mina meets my eyes. *Bam.* Yes. Energy transfer. We smile.

Now poli-sci guy's lecturing her about the influence of the Misogynists on a band he heard once in Brooklyn who *were kind of lame but it was interesting how they appropriated your ferocious textuality, like Le Tigre but less cerebral and more melodious than Sleater-Kinney.* She looks like she wants to stick a knife into her ear. Maybe I'm projecting. Poli-sci guy's wife is riveted. Her wordless stare makes it look like she's on acid.

Mina sticks out a hand to me.

Hey. Mina.

We emailed about Crispin and Jerry's. Ari.

Oh, right. Hey. Warm, genuine. Emanating the ballyhooed glow. I never get over the wild spectacle of pregnancy. It's so outside of time. So elemental. So (fuck it) sacred. Who'd really think twice about those Manson kids murdering Sharon Tate? Yet another slashed-up chick: next. Poor thing was pregnant, though, so bona fide atrocity forever.

We're gonna get some more drinks, Poli-Sci says abruptly. The wife follows.

Jesus fuck, Mina whispers when they're gone.

I love her. Mellow people always seem slightly melancholic, don't they? Whenever I stop grinning for five seconds in a social setting, someone always asks me what's wrong.

Cat breaks the spell to ask if we've seen the highbrow TV of the moment.

Oh my God! Betsy hollers from the kitchen. *I hear it's amazing! Is it amazing? We just got Season One. I hear it's amazing!*

It's amazing.

Okay, so I have to watch it. I'm really excited. Everyone says it's amazing.

It is. It's amazing.

This is as close as they ever come to talking about anything.

But Mina's looking at me.

Is Ari short for something?

Ariella, I say, with loathsome girly twist. In college, reading Plath, I unofficially changed it to Ariel, and felt immediately tougher, braver, like I might someday find the courage to kill myself. But the lie slid from grasp, as lies do. And I'll never have remotely the courage to kill myself.

Pretty, she says, and tries in vain to take a deep breath; no easy task what with fetus cutting into lung capacity.

You must be thinking about names?

She shrugs.

When are you due?

Last week.

Wow.

Yeah. She holds up her right hand and turns it slowly around, marveling at swollen fingers.

I gulp wine, impatient to get where I'm going, wine-wise.

Such a mindfuck, right? Can't sleep? Weird dreams? Sciatica, indigestion? Peeing constantly, sick of being told to, like, "enjoy this time"? And people don't seem to trust that you'll let them know when you've had the baby, right?

Oh my God, it's like, people: I will let you know when I've had the fucking baby. You don't have to ask me every motherfucking day if I've had the baby.

I confess: *Mine just turned one.*

Yeah, Crispin and Jerry told me. Midwife says I can try castor oil in the next couple of days.

A midwife! My throat catches. She's no fool.

Listen, do you think I've done my duty here? I need to go home, like, ten minutes ago. My entire body is sort of throbbing. You know?

Totally.

She downs the last bit in her glass, beams at me.

What do you have? Boy or girl?

Boy.

What's his name?

Walker.

That's a good name.

I nod and sputter something about letting me know if she needs anything and *good luck.* Oh right, luck. Like you'd offer a mountaineer heading out into the Nepalese dawn, never to return.

Be bold and mighty forces will come to your aid, another glass of wine might trumpet through me. Of course a midwife. No one's going to cut Mina Morris open like a fucking lab-rat piece of trash; she's not the type. She's gonna do it like for real do it. The goddesses are with her! Hang tough, sister. No way out but through!

Like I know shit about the way through. I pour myself another to ease the burgeoning wine migraine. Lose patience with a few conversations. Close talker with pork breath, painter who cannot fucking remember my name even though we've met like a hundred times, French bitch in her Kabuki makeup and torture shoes, Jewish studies ass (*wonderful to see you, Ariella!*).

Go upstairs to find the bathroom, wander into the bedroom. Close the door, make myself at home. Nothing of note in Cam and Betsy's drawers.

I always imagined faculty social politics as some intellectually deranged orgiastic laser show, everyone sleeping with everyone, forging strange alliances over years of close quarters, one big incestuous Machiavellian psychodrama. All these potent, messy minds reading Foucault on futons on the floor with other people's spouses, lit by vintage modern paper lanterns in otherwise empty rooms. Maybe a jade plant, maybe a ficus. Talking through problems of philosophy, the meaning of life, the nature of morality, the *way things are,* dispensing with bullshit and superficiality. Like the moodiest, smartest, funniest, sexiest soap opera ever, with a *great* soundtrack. Enclaves of special beings, exempt from the rules of the workaday world, talking about things that *matter,* in so doing, mattering themselves. Like artists but better, because artists are ideally super-duper crazy and/or must die young.

But it's nothing like that. No one's having any sex whatsoever. It's polite and competitive and stilted and pretentious and self-conscious and humorless, everyone blowing half-heartedly, protectively, on the tiny ember of whatever it was that originally sparked any actual interest or passion. All bitter about grading and meetings and students, talking about absolutely nothing. Bunch of insular self-styled martyrs, and to what?

Paul finds me a minute or an hour later, sprawled fast asleep on Cam and Betsy's bed. *You think they fuck here?* I wonder aloud, rousing.

He doesn't answer. I'm in trouble.

Most fun I've had in a while.

I was pretty much your big round regular happy pregnant lady. Do you realize how *nice* everyone is to pregnant ladies? (Mansons excluded.) Nothing ironic about it; no way to downplay the honest-to-goodness-ness. I grew big, full of life. No irony. Not an iota. Not an iota of an iota.

I mean, fine, there were one or two moments of acute oh-shit-this-is-really-happening. But those moments did not undermine the honest-to-goodness-ness, not one bit.

Got slow and uncomfortable and slower still and even more uncomfortable and eventually impatient. Started to think I'd be pregnant forever. Paul got on my nerves. Certainly it would've been nice to have a woman around. Sister, mother, aunt, cousin, friend. Perhaps the absence of any began to crackle and hum, low at first, barely audible static. Maybe I mistook it for the white noise of the womb, persistent reminder of the magic therein. By the time I realized things were not going well, things were so far from well.

Okay! All right. High time to call the baby by name. More than a year old and still I go on about "the baby." He babbles agreeably to himself, holds an old toothbrush aloft. He likes to offer to brush your teeth for you. He's obsessed with a book about a toothbrush cowboy named Charley. His chatter sounds like talk but is not quite talk. My father and stepmother Sheryl, our visitors, observe him closely.

Lot of autism these days, Sheryl notes, forehead tensed where not in elective nerve paralysis. *Shouldn't he be* [whatever the fuck all my friends' grandchildren are doing] *by now?*

Walker! my dad shouts, holding up a cheese stick or a toy, or talking into a banana as if it were a phone. *Walker, come here! What is your name? Do you know your name?* Walker just grabs the bribe, disregards the crazy old man, cruises away. In this I am assured he is perfectly bright.

Sheryl calls us "artsy kids" because we live up here, wear functional shoes, are of reproductive age, ride bikes. She thinks I'm a real estate visionary because I moved into a shitty apartment in a shitty neighborhood in Brooklyn in 1999. She regularly directs my attention to media mention of Brooklyn. *Look, a new restaurant in BROOKLYN! It's very HIP now, apparently.*

They relish grandparenthood, or some projection of

grandparenthood, like they relish a shortlist of life's offerings: fundraisers of every stripe, anything to do with the Holocaust, whatever's showing at the Jewish Museum, grossly overdressing for rousing High Holiday sermons in which they are beseeched to solve world Jewry's problems, past and present, by sending money to Israel and voting Republican if it comes down to it.

They have "forgiven" us for not having Walker circumcised, though Sheryl recoils from diaper changes as though in protest.

Sheryl runs an organization that promotes Jewish books. Books about Jewish mothers, daughters, fathers, sons, reclaiming Yiddish, moving to Israel. Bread-and-butter books about the one and only genocide, my favorite of which is, I kid you not even a little, *The Holocaust Survivors' Cookbook*. Books about children of Survivors and books wondering at the emotional well-being of children of children of Survivors. Books about Jews who marry non-Jews, Jews who abhor the marrying of non-Jews, Jews ambivalent about being Jewish, people or entities accused of not liking Jews and/or Israel. Humor books about Jews who undereat/overeat, Jews who date online. Swoony debut novels of mystical redress for gassed lovers. Literary doorstops in which unlikely entities—bowling, Zionism—are united in metaphor. Post-apocalyptic sagas in which there is Only! One! Jew! Left! In! The! World!

It's all a little up its own butthole. And the thing is, Sheryl hasn't read a whole lot of like anything else. I mean, lady's not so well acquainted with Malamud or Bellow. She doesn't know who Gertrude Stein is. She's never heard of Paul Celan.

She often gets fiction and nonfiction confused. When Philip Roth won the Pulitzer, she shook her head vehemently: *self-hater.*

My father is Ophthalmologist to the Stars. Immediately (and I do mean immediately) after my mother died he married a social-climbing German émigré ten years his junior with a thing for Jews (o-ho, they love us now, don't you know), but that ended within a year when he realized he had married a social-climbing German émigré fourteen years his junior with a thing for Jews. And of course it turned out Astrid wanted to have children, whereas I guess old Norman felt he was done with the having of children. Astrid spoke of converting to Judaism but made no progress toward this end. She had the sharpest jawline I've ever seen. We didn't have much in common, Astrid and I, though she was given to offering me stagy hugs when my father was around. My father, the blind ophthalmologist.

She hates me, I once heard Astrid say, weeping, through the wall.

Give it some time, darling.

No, Norman. She hates me, Norman. She hates me.

I was fifteen, glad my mother's whole dying rigmarole was over with, ready to move on, ready for life to begin. I didn't hate Astrid. Hate requires love. Also, hello, classic stepparent mistake: it's not about *you.*

Then, *bam,* a matter of months after Astrid disappears, Norman runs into a woman he remembers vaguely from high school in the Bronx, and wow, they've reconnected and hey, isn't it amazing how life brings you back around to people and Arlene's separated with a sixteen-year-old daughter, Lindsay. They took us to lunch at Rumpelmayer's in the spring. Seriously, I shit you not at all: *Rumpelmayer's*. For ice cream sundaes with cherries on top, though we were both already wearing tampons, and Lindsay was rehearsing her first fellatio.

I like your sweatshirt, she said.

The translation of which, if you aren't fluent in Girl, is: I won't try to ruin your life if you won't try to ruin mine.

Thanks. Cool shoes.

Deal.

Arlene and Norman beamed, pretended to examine their menus. That love story lasted about six months before Arlene decided to get back together with her husband, Lindsay's father. Lindsay said they pretend the whole thing never happened.

Then came a few years of the saddest dating you've ever seen. Then the Internet came along and at last he found Sheryl. The Internet! Palace of miracles. They seem happy. I'm glad. She's got two greasy forty-something sons in Westchester I've met like three times total; I get their wives and kids mixed up. One's Lauren, one's Fiona. And they have little Cayden Hayden Jaden Braedons.

Sheryl insists they get on the road before dark. Sheryl hates coming up here, hates driving, is convinced that driving in the dark is akin to putting a loaded gun in your mouth.

Love you, Daddy.

Think about Thanksgiving.

I will.

Maybe we'll come up next weekend.

No, Norm, dinner with Jody and Harry next weekend.

Tomorrow, incidentally, is seventeen years since we buried my mother. My father doesn't mention it. I can't tell if he thinks about it and won't talk about it or if in fact he doesn't think about it at all. And I don't say anything about it either, so.

You okay? Paul asks. Unspooling floss. He knows he's required to ask when he senses that I am, in fact, not. It's sort of cute, how jumpy and tentative he gets when he has to inquire about my emotional state, like I'm the possible explosive device and he's the military German shepherd.

I spit toothpaste into the sink. *Anniversary.*

It'd be creepy if he kept track, but I'm weirdly hurt he's unaware. Comes around every year, and we've been together for what, now, three? It's like, don't make me say it, okay? Just stick your proverbial tit in my proverbial mouth, make me feel better. Curl up next to me like a faithful pet, stay close, breathe. Tell me a joke, bring me chocolate and some tea, kiss me, rub my back, make me laugh, wrap your arms around me good and tight, shut up and stay close.

It dawns on him. *Your mom.* He approaches with his arms open. *Oh, babe.*

It's fine, I say, because it's not like I'm reminded she's dead or newly sad she's dead or anything as simple as that. She's always dead, and time does a pretty good job on whatever the hell that means. It's more like I get yanked back into the shit, forever eleven, twelve, thirteen, caught in the fray. Not logical. No explaining it.

It's a spiral, I tell him. *It's the eye of the tornado. It's time and space inverted in a nightmare. It's being trapped in a mine.*

Of course he doesn't get it. How could he? His hundred-and-two-year-old grandfather just got upgraded to the wing of the nursing home from which you leave in a bag, and that's the worst of it in his family so far.

He gives me that look, the one he always gets just before he suggests I go get a massage or treat myself to a day of galleries and boutiques in Hudson or *maybe it's time to see someone, Ari; maybe you need some help.*

Useless.

Wonder if Mina's given birth. Maybe I'll knock on her door with a plate of baked goods—vegan pear almond cinnamon, say, though I've never successfully baked jack in my life. She'll be in early labor, dancing, some Neil Young on, sage burning, a party, a happening, her friends over, a circle. Raft of women, Mina in the middle, and they'll invite me in, tell me to stay, and help, join the circle. We'll move together around her in some primal dance called forth from anonymous foremothers, the ones who came before the ones who came before the ones who came before.

We'll calm and soothe her—*mmm-hmmm, yes,* we'll say, *yes, yes, good, good*—hold her all the way through, share in the sweat and strain and glory. Unwavering, unflinching, rooted, brave. We'll accomplish the impossible act and emerge sisters.

Can't sleep. Raccoon or squirrel or whatever is moving around in there, scratching at the insides of our walls. *Thump, knock, thump.*

Kind of silly to keep pretending I have a dissertation in the works. Anything at all in the works.

My mother's mother was prone to miscarriage. She had a bunch, I don't know how many. More than a few. Maybe it was genetic, maybe it was war trauma, maybe it was psychic, maybe the Good Lord in His Infinite Wisdom simply did not want her bearing children, not after what she had been through, what she had survived.

Finally, pregnant with my mother at the advanced age of thirty-two, she was prescribed a miracle drug. Even better: an *experimental* miracle drug. Diethylstilbestrol. DES, for short. Some kind of synthetic estrogen. (Hey, listen, rule of thumb? The minute anyone says "miracle drug," run. Especially if it's a *lady-specific* miracle drug, dig? Opt the fuck out, please. Stay away. They have no idea what they're doing to you, and they Really Do Not Care.)

So it did indeed prevent miscarriage, good old DES, but in so doing also—oh yeah, oops, by the way, sorry!—fated the unborn to all manner of cancerous disaster. DES Daughters, they're called. Too soon to tell whether we Daughters of Daughters will have what are euphemistically referred to as "indicators," but hey, I'm on the edge of my fucking seat.

Every few years I get a packet from the CDC. A big white eight-by-ten envelope with their logo: *Safer·Healthier·People.* It's vaguely sinister how they track me down, my little epidemiological parole officers.

The first packet landed in my college mailbox freshman year. I mumbled something to a Health Center doctor about it, gravely offered up the packet, mumble mumble *DES* something *mother died* mumble *cancer* mumble.

Probably meaningless, the doc said, and shrugged, glancing through the packet. (My mother, dead of medical-establishment hubris. Meaningless? Oh. Okay.)

Then she offered me that pill where you get your period

only four times a year. *It's new,* she practically squawked, *and wonderfully convenient!*

I yearn to one day rip open a CDC envelope and find a different kind of letter. An *on behalf of the entire community, our sincerest apologies for the shortsightedness and carelessness with which we treated the reproductive health of your forebears . . . our bad . . . promise to stop fucking with you ladies,* et cetera.

Anyway then of course my mother had a nearly impossible time getting pregnant herself. The DES Daughters stuff was just coming out, all those shockingly deformed reproductive organs, wow, who knew? So they had to assume it wasn't going to happen, had no choice but to be okay with it not happening, IVF still mostly a science-fictive question mark, though that first freak guinea pup in England was born the very same year. My parents had been married a while and made their peace. A lot of DES Daughters, it turned out, were in the same boat. My mother's deformed reproductive organs turned out to be functional, but barely, and on a short fuse, so to speak. The cancer made itself known six months after—surprise—I was born.

Will's trap has done its thing. Hurrah. A squirrel quivers in it all morning, petrified. Like the baby when we brought him home from the hospital. I stare at him, he stares back. Old/new face, death-wary but fresh. Are we blinking? Are we breathing? What now? I feel bad for him. The squirrel and newborn Walker, too. What a predicament, being here, alive. It can only end badly.

Will picks up the trap with these huge thick canvas gloves, puts it in his truck. We sit on the stoop.

He accidentally brushes the side of my thigh, and there's a current there, of course there is, just how it goes, we're all grown-ups here. After a while he speaks.

How's writing?

Whatever.

I actually have no idea what you're writing about.

Me neither.

He waits.

Girls, I say finally. *I'm getting my PhD in Algorithms of Girl.*

He is prepared to take me seriously, and what a gift that is. So the least I can do is take myself seriously for the moment.

I wrote this thing for my master's about how feminist organizations very frequently tend to implode and it got published in this journal nine people read and so I got this fellowship to turn it into my dissertation and I sort of went with it.

There's a great series of row houses opposite us. Beige, navy, dark green, burgundy. Contrasting trim on each. A bunch of people had wanted that fellowship. Good for me.

So why do feminist organizations implode?

Because women are insecure competitive ragey cuntrags with each other. In a nutshell. A lot of the records of some of the better-known ones are, like, in archives. Women in women-only groups just rip each other to shreds.

He laughs. Then I laugh, which feels like clean air, spring water. It's not until you laugh again that you realize you have not laughed in a long-ass time.

I used to be really into, like, Adrienne Rich, and Andrea Dworkin—God, Andrea Dworkin. I'm this little radicalized undergraduate dyke freak screaming myself hoarse at Ani DiFranco shows, and next thing you know I'm blazing through a master's, now I'm in line for a doctorate.

That's pretty cool.

I guess, except I don't care anymore. My advisor's pretty much given up on me, and soon the fellowship will run out and I can stop pretending, like, just admit that it's a bust and I'm not up to it. Then I have no idea what to do with myself. Maybe have another baby. This is meant as a joke, and I say it all mocking, stupid-like. But it's so not funny, I'm dizzy.

I pick up a piece of forgotten yellow sidewalk chalk and scribble. It's not until you really talk to someone that you realize how infrequently you actually talk to anyone. I feel like Will *likes* me, weirdly enough. Paul does exquisite fucking, problem solving, logistics. Paul follows instructions. Paul is an excellent driver. Paul makes sure we don't bounce checks. But Paul does not necessarily keep me company. And who can blame him?

Will lights a cigarette. I reach for a drag. This is the longest conversation we've ever had. The drag is a mistake.

I think I, ah, sort of lost my mind this year?

Ha ha ha ha ha. Ha ha ha ha ha ha!

Yeah, he says finally. *I think a lot of women go through that.*

What, abandon their dissertations?

Lose their minds. Having a kid.

Sitting on this here stoop requires my full attention. The second drag is also a bad idea. It's windy and cold and I'm not wearing a hat or gloves. My nose is running.

Thanks for the squirrel assist.

No problem.

We could climb into his truck and drive until we hit the

farthest ocean, never come back. Things like that have been known to happen.

Instead we go inside. I offer tea, which he declines, like I'm trouble.

Sorry, I say, out of nowhere.

No, he says, leaving. He's wearing a gray plaid flannel shirt and it's the same gray as his eyes, goddamn it.

She was not beautiful, my mother, but is remembered as such, small recompense for dying young.

My father, when pressed to talk about her, admits she was "moody." Which is deeply hilarious, like all euphemisms.

Bitch from hell, I scrawled in my diary at nine. Made her only child call her Janice. Used physical force and terror for shits and giggles. Paid someone else to care for her child and treated that person horribly.

In a fine mood she might take me shopping or out for ice cream, host dinner parties with a half-insane, vivacious gleam in her eye. In darker moods she'd scowl to bring down the house, rage, take to bed for days, say terrible things to my father and to me. If she was angry, if she was sad, you were going to suffer. The darkness is most memorable, far outweighs the decent. The malevolent fog.

She abused our housekeepers, made them cry. She preferred Hispanic housekeepers to black ones, because the black ones didn't take shit. The Hispanic ones took her shit like real professional shit takers, just how she liked it.

I remember a succession of terrified, kowtowing brown women: *yes Miss Janice, okay Miss Janice, I so sorry Miss Janice, oh Miss Janice yes I so sorry.* She'd give them a raise whenever they survived an abusive episode, then ultimately fire them over something insignificant. A parade of crying brown women ran from our apartment. Some gave me kisses on their way out. Spanish benedictions; I was their little *pobrecita.* One pressed her lips to my forehead.

Sweet girl, sweet girl, bye. I be praying for you.

It's true, too, though, that Janice made chocolate chip cookies once in a while, and let me lick the batter off the beaters, so she wasn't all bad.

She wore tiny gold hoop earrings. She once got a perm (big mistake). She loved the movies. She relished her movie popcorn like nothing you've ever seen relished. She consumed culture. Saw every exhibit. Was passionate about everything. Read every book. I understood early that I'd find what I needed in books, if not in her. She gave me that.

But the baby. The baby. I am not saying enough about the baby. Walker. Him: a person! My son. His own person. Swell little guy. Sunny super-lovely love of a guy. If I kill myself, maybe he'll grow up to be a poet.

In the first days I suffered spontaneous letdown, which sounds like a fascinating psychological disorder but really means there was milk absolutely everywhere. Sopping wet all of the time. Constantly shoving cloth diapers down my shirt. A big old leaky funereal fountain, that was me. He'd latch onto one side, and the other would just spray. I had to start nursing him lying down so gravity could slow it.

He wouldn't sleep. I felt convinced that the surgery had damaged him, ruined his chances for a happy way in the world. He was always hungry. He needed to be held, he needed to nurse. He shat his diaper, he pissed his diaper. He cried, he needed to be held, he needed to nurse. Endless need.

I did not understand how there could be no break. No rest. There was just no end to it. It went on and on and on. There was no end. And I couldn't relinquish him to Paul, not for a minute, because he was *mine*, you see, *mine, my* baby, *my* responsibility, mine alone. I had to stand guard over him, make sure he was safe and okay and breathing and loved and fine and very close at hand. There was an agony that bordered on physical when he wasn't in my arms. Every cell screamed No! Murder! Where is he? Hold him close! Hold him tight! Don't let go!

Way more physically exhausting than I could have imagined. Just the sheer physicality of it, especially agonizing after surgery. Was the baby difficult because the mother was having a difficult time, or was the mother having a difficult time because the baby was difficult?

He refused sleep. Sleep, why wouldn't he sleep? When might he sleep? We needed to sleep. All of us, sleepless. Lie down now and sleep. Nothing made sense. Sleep. Sleep. Sleeeeep.

So it was that, after a tearful phone call to my father—*an extra pair of hands,* I begged, *we just need an extra pair of hands here*—he and Sheryl parked themselves in the living room, held the baby, took endless photos of themselves and each other holding the baby.

A few times they took breaks to berate us about circumcision.

You're making a terrible mistake, my father said, addressing himself mostly to Paul. And to me: *you have no idea what it's like to grow up in boys' locker rooms.*

We've had enough with the knives for now, Dad, thank you.

Sheryl was likewise appalled. *They have no respect! Millions dead in the camps, and they can't be bothered to circumcise their son.*

My father shook his head sadly. *It's the one thing even barely observant Jews can respect.*

Don't bother, Norm. She's just doing it to get a rise out of us. He's going to have to do it later, when it's incredibly painful.

Paul, usually generous and silent around them, piped up. *Actually it's been shown to be incredibly painful for an infant, too.*

Oh bullshit! Sheryl's face could not convey displeasure. Or pleasure, for that matter. *One tiny snip and they don't feel a thing, it's so quick.*

We disagree.

Well, of course it means nothing to you. *It's not* your *heritage.*

I sat there trying to nurse, half hiding myself in shame and abasement. My father was obviously uncomfortable with my exposed tits, wore a stupid transparent look of disgust, and left the room whenever possible to avoid looking at me.

Sheryl lost herself in her device. The kettle was on for tea. The kettle began to scream.

A woman in a room has as many people to take care of as the number of people in that room, Marianne once wrote. I underlined it.

Water's boiling, Sheryl noted, but didn't move.

Fall's given way entirely now. The trees are bare, and daylight's deeply unsatisfying. Tried to get away with one more day wearing just a sweatshirt and am freezing my ass off.

Walker's at Nasreen's, I'm working the co-op. Midday you got your retirees, your local fucked-up art kids, your welfare folk, your moms from the suburbs, because organic is best.

I take a break and have a cup of tea by the info desk. I keep thinking I'll make friends here, but something's wrong with me or something's wrong with this place or both, because I have made not a one.

Walker cried again today when I dropped him off at Nasreen's. I fail him and fail him and fail him.

Few feet away a brand-newborn in a carrier on the ground. Its mother is trying to make a decision about bananas. Folded-up kitten, blinking, blobby. Rosebud. Raw.

Who can relax with that thing nearby? My jaw gets hard, extremities cold. Knot in my shoulder, have to remind myself to breathe. It's weird when people jiggle and coo those balls of undercooked human. It's weird to see them in public. Turn off the lights! Turn down the music! Get on your goddamn knees, beg pardon, avert your eyes, face to the earth, pray.

When I see pregnant women, I want to take them by their shoulders and shake. I mean *shake.* Are you ready? No, not have you decided on your child's name and gender and aesthetic! No, not do you have every possible medical procedure lined up! I mean are you *ready!?* Like spiritually, bitches. Spiritually.

Finally, at wits' end, desperate one cold early evening, I knocked on Crispin and Jerry's door with newborn in the sling. Paul was at office hours, late. Paul was always somewhere, doing something. Paul was still a part of the world. Paul was still in possession of his body, mind, spirit. It felt like he was avoiding me. I had begun to hate him a little because I wished badly to avoid myself, too.

They'd always been friendly, Crispin and Jerry. A pie when we moved in; a polenta casserole when we got home from the hospital. I thought I'd say thank you in person for the casserole, which was so very delicious.

When Jer opened their door he was laughing at something Crisp was saying. Their house was bright and warm and smelled, I am not joking, of fresh bread. Rickie Lee Jones was doing a particularly jazzy number on the stereo.

His face fell the second he saw me.

Are you okay?

Thank you for the polenta. I forgot your dish, I'm sorry. I washed it.

That's okay. You're welcome. Want to come in?

I don't know, I'm kind of losing my mind? A foreign keening in my voice. Walker asleep on me, bundled in my coat.

Come in, sweetie.

I'm sorry. I just need. I don't know. Can I just hang out here for a little while? I don't mean to bother you guys. If you're busy. Because our house is . . . I'm just kind of losing my mind? You know what I mean? Are you guys, like, super busy?

Rickie Lee was bebopping, and Crisp shook his hips to show me how busy they were.

Yes, honey, we are absolutely swamped.

They fed me. They murmured and giggled over the baby. They threw this impromptu intimate little party, then sent me on my way a few hours later feeling almost human, almost whole.

What r u doing for dinner Jerry would text a few times a week, which became a simple **come over,** which gave way to my simply going over.

Always something on the stove, something in the oven. Something from the CSA, fresh, local, seasonal. Jerry a phenomenal cook, a humble and relaxed natural. And as the days got brighter and longer—baby rolling over, sitting up, cutting teeth, eating applesauce—I settled into something a little like okayness, and I thought: maybe I'm better. Maybe I'm okay.

One night Jerry handed me a joint after dinner, and Crispin produced a lighter.

Good medicine, he said. I hadn't had any since before the baby, since before we moved up here. I had no source, and figured: okay, let's try life without. But now I was no longer pregnant. And life wasn't really working so well without.

I looked at the baby, passed out on a blanket on the floor.

He's fine, Jerry said. *We'll open some windows.*

I mean, breast milk?

Crispin put his arm around me.

Sweet pea, I have to believe your mental state right now is the most dangerous thing for that kid. Anything that can help you relax is probably for the best. They already gave him a big ol' payload of serious painkillers at birth, right? This is a silly little herb. Don't worry about it. Seriously. Here.

Okay. I was home. I laughed until I cried. Laughter a transfusion. Oh my God. I'd missed this so much. A thousand hardened deposits melted away. God, had I missed this. It felt like easing into a hot bath, my first exhale. Rains after drought, and so on. I had been, it turned out, rather severely clenching my jaw.

Crisp told of family, how they rejected him when he came out. Unnatural, they said. Shameful. They didn't have a lot of money. Dad in the navy. Mom taught home ec until home ec got phased out. It was really his dad with the serious homophobia, but the mom couldn't, wouldn't stand up to the dad.

I guess they'll both be gone pretty soon, Crisp said.

His sister kept in touch with him off and on.

I mean, I get Christmas cards. The sister was a bit of a problem for the parents, too, remaining unmarried until past forty, at which point, finally married, she was unable to produce children. At which point the parents offered their life's savings—earmarked for a bunch of cruises—and said: make a baby.

All winter we went on like that, and through the spring, and summer, too, until they went away, those jerks.

It's always that way with periods of crisis: people you expect and want to be there for you are incapable and/or unwilling, and others you never imagined would be there for you show up with exactly what you need, exactly how you need it. And there is almost no way, alas, no way at all, to predict which people will be which.

Got my period for the first time since Walker. (*Aunt Flo's coming to town!* my friend Molly used to holler when she started to feel insane and sad and achy, when a massive pimple showed up on her otherwise perfect chin.)

Realized something was up yesterday, when I read in the paper about a six-year-old boy in Glens Falls accidentally shooting himself in the head with his friend's stepfather's gun. Which was of course loaded, in an unlocked cabinet. They're always loaded in an unlocked cabinet, somehow. Always the friend's stepfather's gun. There was a picture of the little boy, wearing glasses. Huge, unselfconscious, gap-toothed grin. An involuntary sob rose up in me and echoed through the house.

Paul came in with the baby.

Are you okay?

No. This little boy shot himself.

He glanced at the headline, at the picture.

Surprising it doesn't happen more often, I guess. Paul and the baby and the dead little boy stared at me.

No, I'm fine. I mean, everything's just swell, Paul. I mean, how does the world even continue to spin, you know? How is it so fucked-up easy to die and so fucking hard to get born? How is that kind of imbalance possible? You know? What is a possible explanation for that? Can you explain that to me? I would really like someone to explain it to me. I mean, what the fuck? *Someone had to give birth to that boy. What the fucking FUCK?*

He handed me a tissue.

Why don't you go take a nap or something?

The little boy in the paper just grinned.

Some other things about my mother.

She liked burnt toast with margarine on a square of paper towel. She once threw a chair at a wall when she came home to find me watching TV against orders. A man came to fix the plaster and paint a few days later. The incident was never mentioned again.

She got sick when I was a baby, got better, got sick again in grade school, got slightly better, got sick again, did not get better. I wasn't really in the loop. It's fuzzy. No one told me shit. I had to pick up clues, figure it out. She got sicker and sicker. Dead the November of my seventh-grade year, months still to go before summer vacation, the stench of sickness and death coming off me all mixed up with puberty, that other treacherous decay.

Her photos are all over the place; this house is like a

shrine: black-and-white baby in saddle shoes, blushing bride with bouffant and cinched waist. Strangely quiet in her late thirties, owl glasses reflecting the light from a window as she gazes down at me, newborn in her arms staring blankly back. It's like an unhinged Mexican funeral in here. Even found this weird little painting of a skull at a thrift shop in Troy. All done in fluorescents, trippy.

My father knocked on my bedroom door the night it finally happened.

It's over, sweetheart. It's over. It's finally over. He hugged me tight—too tight—and cried on my shoulder for a while before going out and closing the door behind him, leaving me to my silence and books and female folksingers. Anticlimactic, when it finally happened. I stayed up until dawn, but I couldn't have told you why.

The whole class signed a condolence card. Herd of forced, off-kilter signatures: what pure, distilled humiliation. I had hoped to distinguish myself in other ways. It was embarrassing that my mother had died, that I was so human and pitiable. Everyone was *nice* to me, so false and bright. Her dying had nothing to do with *me*, I wanted to explain. *I* didn't die!

But I had entered a different realm and would have to stay there indefinitely, in close proximity to death. There was an exoticism inherent in that; I just wasn't sophisticated enough to go Goth with it.

I was let off the hook for the Jenny J assault (though her father did briefly, excitedly threaten to sue). I relished the way she cowered from me at school, eye turning from navy blue to purple and red to rot yellow. That's right, bitch. Watch out. She tried to avoid me. I'd stare her down to torture her. It made me feel better.

Teachers spoke to me like I was a frightening robot whom the wrong tone or combination of words might short-circuit. In lieu of talking to me himself (at all, about anything), my father sent me to Jack, inaugural shrink, who squirmed a lot and said *hmmm* and *those are powerful feelings,* eyes darting at the clock over my shoulder.

Here is a little secret about grief, catastrophe, loss, suffering: you are exactly the same after as before. Only more so.

Jack told me not to have feelings about my feelings, advised me to write her a letter and bring it to her gravesite in Queens, tell her all the things I wished I could say.

Sorry you're dead, Mom, I love you the best I could come up with, and a lie.

We decide not to "do" Thanksgiving this year. A relief.

Last year we drove down to the city with Walker in the brand-new offgassing car seat. My incision was still giving me trouble. I was still moving like a ninety-five-year-old. We arrived to find Sheryl and my father and cousin Erica and whoever else doting on the turkey, bobbing and weaving around it like it was made of eternal fucking light, barely able to pull themselves away long enough to greet us. The turkey, the turkey, look at the turkey! Sue me: I'd imagined them making a little fuss over *the baby.* They're real into their juiced-up carcasses, my father and Sheryl. It gets them incredibly excited, ministering to a dead animal.

There are no pictures of me or my mother in that apartment, by the way. Not a one. There's Sheryl's mother's mother in a late nineteenth-century Russian portrait, Sheryl's mother as kid, Sheryl's parents' wedding, Sheryl as sorority president. There are the sons as grade-schoolers, sons and wives on respective wedding days, grandchildren in studio portraits. There's Norman and Sheryl on a group tour, Norman and Sheryl on another group tour, Norman and Sheryl on yet another group tour.

They had made us a salad and a bowl of overcooked greens (*for the vegetarians!*) as though it were a proud meal to offer a post-op nursing mother. Of course they added turkey juice to the stuffing, so I ate the bread and salad and over-sautéed greens and this awful pie one of Sheryl's sons brought from FoodLand. You would not believe the crap Sheryl's greasy sons and their wives call food. The waxy, genetically engineered fruits, the processed shit, the corn syrup dextrose canola preservative crap they call food. That they're not all dead is testimony to general good genes, I guess.

I mostly sat on the couch and nursed, as one nurses and nurses and nurses a newborn. Paul brought me a plate, kept asking if I was okay. At one point Sheryl tried to drape a blanket over me.

Later one of Sheryl's grandkids came over and stood right next to me. She was about six, watching with great interest.

What's he doing? she whispered, peering intently at the baby's tiny working mouth.

He's drinking milk, I whispered back. There was still time for her. She stood stock-still for another moment, then ran over to her mother.

THAT BABY'S DRINKING MILK FROM HER BOOBIE, she stage-whispered, eyes wide. The room burst into laughter.

Yeah, her mother whined in that hellish fake voice people use to bullshit to their kids, *you didn't do that, did you, Hayden?*

Hayden said she guessed not.

My next visitor over on the couch was Erica. Walker had

fallen asleep and released my swollen, still-wet nipple, which I hadn't yet bothered to put away. The face Erica made, you'd think she was looking at a steaming fresh defecation. I pulled the cloth diaper out from under my shirt, where it had been stemming the leak from my other boob, and hooked the nursing bra all up again without waking the sleeping kid, proud of myself for having recently mastered this kick-ass series of moves. As proud as I've ever been of anything, come right down to it.

Erica sat there with that face like she was about to puke, or masturbate, or both. She was blind to the baby—the endlessly fascinating curve of his forehead, his astonishingly perfect nostrils and fingernails and eyelashes. Holding him in your arms reframed all things. How painfully obvious it was that men, with their secret societies and weapons stockpiles, could know little of life. Elsewhere in the room were heated discussions about football and politics and a new sci-fi movie whose effects were, according to one of Sheryl's sons, *off the hook.*

So, Erica said. *Listen. I wanted to talk to you about the wedding?*

Uh-huh, I said. Cipriani, February. Winter Wonderland. She'd been starving herself for the better part of a year. I was supposed to be a bridesmaid, wear a lavender gown. I intended to drink some moderate amount of alcohol for the first time in a long while. This moderate amount was going to get me Super Fucked Up. I was looking forward to it.

Yeah, so, Steve and I really feel that it's our *day, you know?*

Sure.

I mean, what I actually mean is that it's my day, really. It's my day.

Christ. How estranged from yourself, how juvenile and spastic do you have to be to cling to that kind of idea? Like a kid with a behavioral disorder.

And here's the thing. She had rehearsed this. "The Thing." Up it came from the entitlement swamp, covered in reeds, wearing a muddy veil and clutching an enormous bouquet. *So many of our friends have kids. And even though we love kids and love our friends' kids and wish we could include everyone, we've decided we can't have everyone's kids, and it's not fair to make any exceptions, so I just wanted to let you know that we're not going to be having kids at the wedding.* She had definitely rehearsed it; she recited it without pause. *And I just feel that having kids there would just, like, take the focus off me. So!* She took a closing breath, exhaled it noisily.

Erica. I'm nursing. He's a newborn.

She set her jaw, ready to rumble.

We declined to stay the night. On the drive home the baby bawled in the back while I bawled in the front.

I'm really not sure who I should try and comfort first, Paul said.

Fuck you, I said, because he was the only person available.

We pulled in to a rest stop in Ulster County, devoured the most disgusting/amazing heat-lamped pizza ever.

Something's crossed over in me, and I can't go back. (That was Thelma in *Thelma and Louise*.)

Hey, uh . . . sorry to bother you? I'm a friend of Mina Morris's. We're at uh . . . Crisp and Jerry's? The water cut out this morning. The hot water. There's no hot water. And the heat might be on the fritz. We can hear this banging? Can you call us? Thanks a lot.

Male voice. I listen to it three more times. It's pretty amazing that these houses are still standing at all, when you think about it.

Will's happy to see me, I could swear he is. It smells of Nag Champa in there. He gets his coat. We walk. Sunny, freezing.

She's having a baby. Any minute. Like, she might be having it right now.

Cool. You can show her the ropes.

How deep in shit she'd have to be!

The guy who opens Crisp and Jer's door is upper forties, short, wool socks, handsome, glasses, flannel. Self-conscious, you can see it immediately in the clothes, which are just slightly too too. Hates his father, wants to impress his father. Not quite enough self-loathing to cancel out the narcissism. Deeply admires people less materialistic than he, can't quite give up on impressing people more materialistic than he. You grow up among the rich, you become a veritable Jungian psychic where material self-representation is at hand.

Hey, the guy says.

He steps aside to usher us in. Teeth-grindingly cold. A space heater is doing very little to help matters. Mina is bundled so thoroughly in blankets on the couch that at first I don't see she's holding her newborn.

We stare.

They look like hairless rats when they're this new, like soft mechanical dolls. The most riveting, shocking hairless doll rats you ever saw. So intense, what happens when there's a newborn in the room. This negative energy charge, this weird, blessed pall. Difficult not to whisper, tiptoe, nice and easy, forget what you were going to say.

Hi, I say.

Four days ago, she says, not looking up.

So small and tender, shockingly close to nonexistence. It's a whole lot like the dying. It's almost exactly the same. Inspires quiet. I worship babies, it occurs to me. This is what worship does: fucks you all kinds of up.

She gestures at the space heater. *Sort of bad timing.*

How are you? Redundant; I have eyes.

Um. I've been better. I'm okay? She's asking: am I? Her hair is wild.

Will and the guy are standing at attention, like they're at a funeral for someone they barely knew, no idea what's required of them.

Then the guy remembers to introduce himself.

I'm Bryan, he says.

Baby daddy? Boyfriend? Relative?

Ari.

Will.

Hi. Cool.

Will leads the way to the basement. Their footfalls thud on the stairs.

Midwife went home the other night, a few hours after. Said she'd stop by again, see how we're doing. Haven't heard from her, though. Left a message. She picks up her device and sets it back down.

You had him here?

Yeah, she says, like duh.

Where's your family? Or whatever. Are they coming? I feel faint, standing over her. A hundred feet tall. And claustrophobic, like when I was a kid, with the panic attacks. A war zone, this: life and death doing a maddening polka on your soul.

She laughs. Laughs and laughs, shakes laughing, tears up, downright glittery. *My family. My family!* This is the funniest, oddest idea she's ever heard. *My family!* She sighs gratefully, happy for the laugh. Laughter the great transfusion.

Ah, she says, calmer now. *My family.* A bit less crazy-eyed, a pinch more present. She stares at her animate bundle. Shakes her head, grins, bugs out her eyes like a soap actor's interpretation of nuts.

My family!

I sit.

2

DECEMBER

One night, late, almost morning, maybe counted as morning, couldn't say for sure, my mother was next to me on the couch while I nursed.

How do you know if he's getting enough?

He's getting enough.

How do you know?

You just know.

Well. We always knew. We used to microwave your formula.

I sighed, closed my eyes, hoped she might not be there when I opened them again.

What? We didn't know. It fills them up better! He'll sleep longer. Oh my God, you know what else we used to do? Benadryl. What a gift that was. Knocked you out for hours.

She giggled and glanced around at the chaotic mess: was the basket full of clean laundry, or was it dirty? The bowl in which I'd eaten that morning's oatmeal, getting crusty. Dirty dishes stacked in the sink. She raised her brows.

Kill you to tidy up a little?

Don't start with me, Demerol bitch.

What? You might feel better if it wasn't such a pigsty around here.

I stared out the big window, arms tense around Walker. Didn't want to be that way around him, no flash of anger.

Sorry, monkey, I whispered. *It's okay.* How much of the rest of my life would I spend thusly assuring this poor moppet that "it" was "okay"?

Incidentally, you have no right to speak to me that way.

That's how she was: hard and mean until you responded in kind, then wounded, self-righteous.

Soon he was finished on the left side, big boy. I lifted him up, held him close, delicious soft hilarious drunk face, patted his back, and put him to work on the right. We passed weeks this way, he and I, submerged, disoriented, in a twisted sort of contentment. Now I yearn for that time, want to lie with him connected and safe. Memory's a ridiculous bastard.

This is my son, I said, gazing at him to be spared her. *This is Walker. Isn't he beautiful?* The big eyes, so liquid and good. You couldn't help but smile, be filled with the presence of whatever the hell we can all agree on.

That's an idiotic name. Where did you even come up with a name like that? What does that even mean?

It's Old English. It's a great name. Hello? Walker Percy? Walker Evans? She was a lover of books and culture, at least.

You should have named him for me.

I said nothing.

I mean, really.

I wanted this to be a good thing, I hissed. *A fresh start. A new thing.* My heart raced. Walker started to cry. I put him up over my shoulder the way my favorite nurse had shown me, pat pat pat rub rub rub. *It's okay. It's okay it's okay it's okay it's okay it's okay it's okay.* Bluffing.

She cackled.

Riiiight. Hey, how's the dissertation coming, Little Miss Fresh Start? You look hard at work.

Fuck you.

Nice.

This is work.

Walker spit up, looked greatly alarmed, settled back down. *Sorry monkey sorry monkey it's okay monkey shhhhhh. Will you hand me one of those rags?*

I was forever in need of someone to hand me something.

Take a shower! Change your clothes. Jesus. Make yourself something to eat. Any opportunity to fall apart, this one. Have you looked in a mirror lately? What is the big deal, here? Get it together. Honestly.

I just had a fucking baby is the big deal you dead cunt.

She began to moo at me, cracked herself up.

Mooooooooo. She got pretty hysterical, and then was gone. Without ever having handed me one of those goddamn rags.

Shhhh monkey, shhhh it's okay, it's okay, it's okay.

I write to Crispin and Jer about their busted boiler. Crisp replies:

> goddamn motherfuuuuuuuck it all to hell. alright, over it, do whatever u have to do. don't skimp. thought that bitch'd last one more winter. thanks, punky. sorry. miss you. ate a pizze last night u would have had a stroke over. jer sends hugs and is getting fat.

Punky is because I told him I was obsessed with Punky Brewster as a kid.

Turns out the old boiler was installed in 1975. Will and a guy from the superstore are almost done replacing it.

Bryan's in an armchair, staring at his computer. Still have no idea what his role is here.

Hurts just to look at Mina's tits, so swollen. She winces when the baby latches. This is the part no one talks about, the part that feels suspiciously like a secret. Sorry: *a* part. And secrets are by nature shameful. Pisses me off, watching her struggle and wince like that.

Look at the teeny-tiny baby, I tell Walker, who nods solemnly and is off again to empty the bottom kitchen drawer of its contents, hurl them one by one to the floor, and put them all away again. So long as he's not in mortal danger.

I bring Mina a glass of water.

She thanks me as though such kindness is going to push her over an edge.

Fuck, my tits hurt so much. They're enormous, her tits, big and hard, like implants.

The baby's name, she's pretty sure, is Zev.

I'm sitting with it, she says. *It feels right. Doesn't it?*

Naming something is almost impossible. Zev sounds pretty good to me. Sometimes I think: Walker!? What the fuck? But when you're used to something it stops mattering, by definition.

I like it, I say. *It's a good name.*

She dabs some ointment on the left. Bryan looks up from his screen to watch.

It's Wolf. Feels right. It jives. I looked at him when he came out, after all my howling, and there he was. She does a soft, melodious howl. *Right? Right, little wolf? I could call him Wolf, I guess. If Zev is too, like, "oooh look at me I'm so Hebrew-y." Maybe Wolf is better.*

I don't think it's too look at me I'm so Hebrew-y.

What's wrong with Hebrew-y? Bryan wants to know, but doesn't look up from his machine.

She just needs us to sit with her. Process. Not so terrifically much to ask. Not so big a thing.

We're supposed to have mothers, I say. *We're supposed to have sisters. But what if you don't have a mother? What if you don't have a sister?*

Or a crappy mother, Mina mutters, massaging a huge, tender tit. *Or a crappy sister.*

All fixed, Will says, clomping back up the basement stairs with the guy from the superstore behind him.

JIM, says the embroidered name tag. Jim tells us his wife just had a baby, too. *Our sixth,* he says. Mina looks horrified and Jim says something about blessings of Jesus.

At which point I gather up my own little blessing, 'cause it's getting late and you should always leave before people want you to.

Call me, I order her. *I can be over whenever.*

She nods solemnly.

The worst part of the Erica wedding fiasco was that she was marrying *Steve,* for the love of antiperspirant! *Steve* was the culmination of her greatest ambition. Not a bad guy but Steve is nothing to get excited about, unless it's excited you don't have to hang out with him too often. He talks a lot about the fancy cocktail bars he can get you into, the epic hotel upgrade he got last time in Vegas, a case of the "meat sweats" he got in some very special restaurant in Argentina once.

I was given a swatch of pale violet fabric, instructed to have a dress made. She was insanely giddy. She was out of her freaking mind.

And so we left the three-month-old to a bottle with a stranger, and I put on the hideous dress, still packing an extra thirty pounds. No metaphor required to describe how awful I looked. No, I'm not one of those women who's figured out how to transcend vanity. Not one of those extraordinarily beautiful women who've figured out how to transcend vanity.

I could have opted out. I could have said no.

Have you ever been to a wedding? Then you've been to every wedding. The bridesmaids like Stages of a Woman's Life dolls. The skinny, working-it single girl, trying hard to not despair her singleness. She looks "good." She sprang for a spray tan. Her lotion has glitter in it. She tries more and more of the magazine tips as she gets older. She's starting to go a little hard around the jaw, there's some sun damage on her hands, and her feet crammed into those stilettos look like a couple of veiny shar-peis, but hey, she's working it. She'll have a few drinks too many. It will become clear she thinks she's in a romantic comedy about bridesmaids. She will fuck one of the groomsmen. Which will it be?

Then there's the pregnant one, smug as hell, all like, looooook, I'm pregnant! I'm so fulfilled and glowy! I've really done it! The single girl and the pregnant girl assiduously avoid each other unless it's to simultaneously, speciously condescend. They feel *so* sorry for each other.

Then the one who's just recently had a baby or two. [Curtsy.] She has that edgy, shell-shocked look, like she's been ripped apart and put awkwardly back together, which, well, she has. But she's still trying, in her sad, half-assed way, despite the fact that the working-it/fabulous phase of her life has ground to a definitive (oh-ho-ho so definitive) halt. She'll never be the same again, she knows. Never, ever. She can barely look at the working-it single girl, who treats her—again with the condescension—like an *elder.* It's precisely when the working-it single girl fails to compete with her that she knows for sure: she is gone. She feels invisible because, in fact, she is! Big animal stuffed into the same dumb dress—maybe it's aqua, maybe it's lime, maybe it's mauve. The pregnant one doesn't want much to do with her but eyes her carefully: she'll certainly not let *her*self go that way.

And then there's the one who's got a couple of bigger kids, school age, pubescents maybe even. She's folded, and it's been a while since. To her these others are sort of cute, embroiled in their struggles. She's done. She could be forty, she could be seventy, makes no difference at all. She is done with her changes. She digs in her heels, ticks off years as they roll on by. She does not sweat the philosophical shit. She does not retread her choices. Worst-case scenario, she is unaware of having made choices. It is what it is. It's done. Nothing left but to rely on prescription drugs for this and that and the other until it's all over for good.

There they are, pretty maids in a row, highlighting one another's failure and ridiculousness, gathered around the lodestar puff-pastry bride. Ushering the bride into *her* next set of shitty options. Grinning plastic grins in the photos uploaded immediately.

We sat at one of those painfully boring couples tables, at which everyone already knew everyone and felt no need to introduce themselves or include us in their conversation, which was inaudible anyhow, given the amplification of the ten-piece band. Fuck you, by the way, couples at couples tables at weddings who don't go out of your way to engage with that one couple who doesn't know anyone.

We left early. My tits were on fire. I did not—ALAS!—get fucked up. And by the time we got back to the hotel my tits were like rocks, like explosive hot rocks, like they were about to rocket right off and explode in a tableau of electric blue and orange. I could feel my tits in my elbows. Walker was sleeping in the porta-crib, and I had to wake him to nurse him, which he tolerated, but then he would not go back to sleep. We sat grimly in a chair by a window until dawn.

Mina, warrior queen. She had her baby at Crispin and Jerry's *house*. She actually *had* her baby.

There are hundreds of clips showing people actually giving birth to babies. You can watch. You've never seen anything so incredible. I watch them all the time. Each completely different. Individuals. No one was going to knife Mina Morris—she's not the type.

The surgery movies are fewer in number and harder to watch. Creepy. Impersonal. I could probably perform one by now.

Why do you keep looking at that stuff? Paul asks. *It only upsets you.*

Maybe I like being upset.

Abdomen cleaned and shaved with an antiseptic solution. Catheter inserted. IV put into arm or hand. General or local anesthetic administered. Patient strapped to the table with arms outstretched, surgical drapes blocking view. Incision across the belly about one to two centimeters above the pre-pregnancy upper border of the bladder. Tissues above the uterus cut and separated. Cut made horizontally into the lower section of the uterus. Amniotic fluid suctioned. Baby pulled out.

Ari. I know it's not what you wanted. But it's over, and we can't change it. So maybe it's time to—

Babies born by C-section often suffer from neonatal respiratory distress often calling for treatment with oxygen therapy in a neonatal intensive care unit. Babies delivered by C-section often have low Apgar scores, usually because of breathing problems, along with lethargy as a result of the anesthesia administered to the mother. These sedatives can also make it hard to breastfeed.

I really wish I understood why you have to keep doing this.

Postpartum endomyometritis, infection of the uterine tissue, is twenty times more likely. The risk of blood clotting is five times greater. Urinary tract infections are common. These infections, usually a result of the urinary catheter, can be treated with antibiotics. Decreased or absent bowel function is also common, usually as a result of pre- and post-surgery narcotics. Women are four times more likely to die from surgical birth than from vaginal birth. Women who deliver surgically can develop scar tissue around the uterus, which can make it more difficult to achieve normal births in the future.

Ari. You have to try and let it go.

Women who deliver surgically are—

Babe. I know.

—thought to suffer from increased rates of postpartum depression, which can include—

What would you like me to do about it, babe? Can you tell me what you want me to do about it?

—feelings of failure, helplessness, posttraumatic stress—

Ari. This isn't helping.

—disempowerment, disappointment, anger, loss, and frustration.

You don't fuckin' say.

At first when she hands him to me it's like I've never held a newborn.

Zev. Squirmy and clenched, like he can tell I'm nervous. They're just little mirrors. They're pure. We don't learn how to lie until around two. The world is no place for these little fuckers, tiny tuning forks. He's way too soft and scary and what if I accidentally kill him? It's totally possible to accidentally kill these things.

But, shit, okay, fine: *Hey baby. Hey Zev.*

How weird he wasn't anything before she made him. Where was he? Somewhere? Nowhere? Now he's here and he has this name and he's a person. Weird. Mina goes to take a shower. I spread a blanket on the floor, swaddle him, that's better.

She comes downstairs steamy, head wrapped in a towel, wearing a fresh T-shirt.

It's a whole new lease on life, she says. *I lost, like, a fistful of hair. Is that normal?*

Completely. Hormones.

Her T-shirt is pink, with a line drawing of a beautiful

woman in an enormous hat, smoking a cigarette. The cigarette smoke forms the word MONTREAL.

I can't get over how normal she seems. Her body. The way she's moving. I mean, huge tits, soft belly; she gave birth a week ago. But here she is, intact. A week post-surgery I was still incredibly fucked up. Gutted like a fish. Hurt to move, but I tried to lay off the painkillers, 'cause they made shitting impossible, then you were supposed to start with the stool softeners. Five days postpartum my incision opened slightly and I had to go back to the fucking hospital, get the sutures reinforced. A fever dream. In the wrong kind of pain entirely. Everything hurt.

Whoa, Mina says. *Where'd you go? You just went somewhere.*

I shake it off, busy myself with finishing touches on a big pot of soup.

Bryan's packing, leaving tonight. I assumed he was the father, the boyfriend. Apparently not.

Friend, Mina says when we're alone. *Off and on. Like a brother. A charming if irritating little brother. I used to tie him up once in a while. Long time ago. He needed a place to stay and I offered. That's his thing: impoverished artist. I hear from him when he needs money, pretty much. He thought it'd be cool to "experience a birth." And because I'm retarded I said okay, sort of half thinking he'd want to, like, "be there for me," which makes me more or less the biggest idiot asshole of all time. Now he's writing about it, apparently.*

Where's he going?

Austin. She rolls her eyes.

Paul's at the library, grading or something. Paul's always somewhere, doing something. Walker's at Nasreen's till five.

This is amazing, she says about the soup.

You're the best, Bryan says, slurping.

Fairy fucking godmother, Mina says.

I'll bring banana bread, witch hazel, fenugreek, arnica, oregano. Swaddles, spit-up rags. A messy lasagna, zucchini bread from the good bakery. Epsom salts, cabbage, belladonna, mustard seed oil. Gelato, raspberry leaf tea. A small piece of rose quartz. Everything she needs.

Bryan gets up to say goodbye when I leave, and gives me a strong hug, a real hug, takes my breath away. It's not until someone really hugs you that you realize how infrequently anyone ever really hugs you.

Pleasure, he says. He's quite the puppy dog.

Later, when Paul gets home, I take a cold, dark, ten-minute walk down to the river. Air feels amazing. Then I clean the kitchen.

You're chipper, Paul observes.

I look up Bryan.

. . . [A]n occasionally profound and important writer, according to some critic. *Trouble is, he publishes quite frequently.*

Think I might actually get out a pen and some Jeanette Winterson before bed. Don't actually do it, but think about it. Which is something.

Today I take Walker to story time at the library and then to the burger place at the mall, because no Nasreen on Thursdays and I get a little panicked without a plan. He has a meltdown in the mall parking lot as I try to load him back into the car seat to go home. Refuses to be put into the seat. You can't reason with them. He just does not want to go in that car seat. He freaks the fuck out about getting into the seat.

I look around helplessly. Nearby, a stranger: white girl with stale bleach job whose three kids are perfectly installed in a seen-better-days blue minivan. Bag upon bag from the mega-store. She watches me. I think: fuck it.

What are you supposed to do when they get like this? I ask her.

They don't pull that shit with me, she says, icy glint in her eye. Then she turns to the kids, lined up in there. *Do you?* Stares them down hard in those stained car seats. They look straight ahead like cadets, lifetimes of stress disorders ahead.

Eight thirty in the morning. Paul and the baby are already downstairs, already finished with breakfast, me as yet unable to get out of bed.

Phone rings. Mina.

Did I wake you? Sorry.

No. What's up?

Bad night. Bad day, then bad night, now . . . just . . . bad.

The light outside's wintry and gray, all shadows, and when I finally manage to get up and over there it's exactly like that inside, too. Heavy. A downshift in key. Like the forest floor. Dark and still and mossy, faintly humming with intensity, scant bits of light filtering through a canopy of high trees. Like no temple that has yet been built. (*Daniel Libeskind is on it,* Crispin would say.) Mugs of tea gone cold are everywhere.

They've been to the pediatrician, and it seems that baby Zev is not gaining weight. He is, in fact, losing weight. The pediatrician is no help.

He was all, "So long as he's peeing, we won't worry. Give him some formula if you're worried. Do you have a new insurance card?"

But she's nursing him constantly and her nipples are

bloody and shredded, there's a giant lump in the lefty, and twenty minutes ago she changed a wet diaper and it was pink. Which means he's dehydrated.

My tits are killing me and he's starving to death and I'm so fucking tired and I am freaking the fuck out. Can you tell? I am freaking the fuck out. And the fucking midwife doesn't return calls.

Are you kidding me? Aren't they supposed to, like, make you placenta soup and sing your praises to the goddesses? Bang a drum or something?

No drum.

It is pretty clear that Zev is failing, in the parlance of infants, to thrive. He looks shriveled, more so even than a couple days ago. Miniature knotted brow. When you're that small, some ounces are a big deal.

She paces and pats, paces and pats. He'll settle for a second or two, but then he's screaming again. That furious impotent infant scream.

It's been like this all night. Okay, okay, shhh. I keep hearing that line? From "A Hard Rain's A-Gonna Fall"? Shhhh, okay. "I saw a newborn babe with wild wolves all around it," you know? Okay, shhhhhh. "I saw a highway of diamonds with nobody on it . . ."

You can't mistake a new mother holding a baby this way, swaying, bouncing on the soles of her feet, babbling like a brook, for anything else. She is speaking in tongues. The baby calms briefly and wails again.

"I saw a newborn babe with wild wolves all around it," she sings softly, emphasis on "wild wolves" the way Dylan does it in this one exquisite slow live bootleg someone gave me once, gravelly voice sliding up and down that line.

And apparently there's something hilarious about all of it, because now she's giggling.

Listen I'm trying pretty hard not to go nuts here and I know it's not really your problem like at all but I haven't slept very much in like a long time it feels like and I really don't know what the fuck to do, I mean the doctor's like "he's fine!" but he's not fine, you fucking cocksucker. Obviously he's not fine! Doctor says "give him some formula if you're concerned." But I'm not giving him fucking formula, fucking prick! He nursed for nine hours yesterday. I kept track. I was sitting in that chair for nine fucking hours, on and off! Nine hours! I had no idea my nipples could hurt this much! And I used to enjoy light S & M! When he latches I can feel it in my eyeballs! Everyone keeps telling me to give the kid a bottle. Give the kid a bottle, give the kid a bottle! I am not giving this fucking kid a fucking bottle! I just birthed him in a fucking bathtub! I am not giving him fucking powder poison cow sugar processed fucking gross Nestlé Africa atrocity sludge! I'm sorry! This is my baby! I am not giving him a bottle! Fuck you very much!

She's trembling the way you do when you've forgotten how to breathe and it hasn't yet dawned on you that you're not breathing.

Baby lets out a wail like the seed of all suffering, and I'm starting to feel a little stressed out myself. That is a seriously hungry baby. My confidence in this matter fills me with a sudden immense pride. That is one hungry-ass baby.

Okay. Let's take a deep breath. I demonstrate: in, out, make her meet my eyes. *I completely, completely get it and it's going to be okay. Have you eaten anything?*

I don't know. Not really. I'm not hungry. I'm not fucking giving him formula, you know? I'm not. Pay attention to what they tell you to forget!

Okay, I say. *Okay.*

Please stop saying that.

Okay. Sorry.

That's Muriel Rukeyser. "Pay attention to what they tell you to forget." You know her?

I think so.

She's great.

Okay.

She tries to nurse again. Breast implants were originally modeled on nursing ones, interestingly enough.

Maybe slide your arm under him a little more, wait, here. Like this. Yeah. So you bring him kind of more straight on. There. Is that better?

It's hideously not better.

I know. It really hurts in the beginning.

I mean, is that, like, it? "It hurts in the beginning"? It's just excruciating, the end? It's supposed to be excruciating? Because it would be nice if I had known anything whatsoever about this before ten fucking days ago, you know? She picks up her phone, throws it down again. *Fucking MIA celebrity midwife bitchrag from hell.* Zev is working hard as he can on her, really concentrating, but it's not working. He's frustrated and she's in agony.

First things first. The pantry. Jerry's fancy Italian dried pasta. Slice and serve an apple while the water boils. Cover the noodles with butter, salt, pepper, grated parmesan, set it down before her. Then I move in right up close, adjust pillows, fold my legs under me, and wait.

Shhh, she sniffles unconvincingly, scarfing the apple. *Shh, shh, shh. It's okay. It's gonna be okay. Okay? It's gonna be okay. Okay? Okay. Okay.*

The word *okay* like a dog treat your consciousness lobs over into the snarling storm of your subconscious. Okay, okay, okay. It's gonna be okay. Okay? Okay? Okay, okay.

But he's wailing again, so hard I can feel it in my own tits again.

Right: my tits.

Obviously: my tits.

My girls. My pups.

Listen, I say. *Can I have him?*

She's confused, but I hold my arms out and nod slowly until she understands. I move so our thighs touch, and take him.

Hello, human seashell. Not Walker. A different baby, new squashed tangle for a face. Tiny gums gleaming as he wails.

Mina goes to town on the pasta.

I lay Zev out on my legs, red-faced and furious, while I liberate my right one.

She's so busy inhaling that pasta, she doesn't register. I look to her for some kind of okay. She stops eating.

You don't have AIDS or anything, do you? People are forever saying dumb things at profound moments; it's the human condition.

No.

She goes back to inhaling the pasta. It's like she's never had pasta.

He's not choosy; he's goddamn hungry. Not the best latch, indeed. Ouch. But there's time, he can learn. Plenty of time, nothing but. He pulls off for a second, the abundance a surprise, and right away he's searching for me again, mouth ajar, panting. Opens wide. Gulp, gulp. Relaxes into me, eyes closed. The whole room goes all melty. Problem solved. All peaceful and blossomy, like after a good first kiss. Unfold. Bask. I remember this. I can do this. Nothing for her to do but watch.

• • •

So yeah, I got cut, but thankfully we got the boob thing right. They wheeled the baby to me in one of those plastic bins. An obstetrical nurse from the NICU followed, her name tag an island in an expanse of bosom. DONNA KENDRICK, RN.

Now listen, honey pie. Here's the deal. Might be tough going in the beginning, but you'll get the hang. And little man here will get the hang, won't you, love bug, and soon you'll be off to the races together. Nothing so easy once you get the hang. You just had a rough start, you guys, but that's over now. Okay? All right. So this is gonna be great. Let's give it a whirl, lemme see what you got. Okay, no, see, you want to bring him straight on, just straight on, give him a good angle so he can do his part. Now does that hurt? Good. It shouldn't hurt. If it hurts, that's a bad latch. A bad latch is no good. A bad latch is bad. So many people, they got a bad latch and they throw up their hands, say it's impossible. They give up. We don't want that. Nothing's so simple once you got the hang. I got four boys, I come up to here on them now. Okay, let's give him another minute like this and then try him out on the other side. Hurts? No. Good. Today you just want to get the gist. This is practice time for you and him; milk's gonna really hit tomorrow, so if you get today right, you'll be off to the races. You just got a look like something hurts. Something hurt? Don't be shy. Right, right, so the trick is we want his lower lip sort of folded open wide as can be, like that, yeah, you see? Yeah, you got it, little man. We're just gonna keep on making sure you get it right, you guys, and by tomorrow you'll be all set, really good to go. Just takes a little practice, a little patience. Okay, let's switch him. Little practice, little patience. Here we go, okay, round two, hey, look at you guys! Perfect. That's good. Good, good. By the time you go home you're gonna be experts. That's what we want. Good. Then you'll be able to enjoy each other. You're going to enjoy each other, you and him, believe me, I swear. You just got a look like you don't believe me. It's a rough road, the C. Not how it's supposed to go. Between you and me these assholes like to know how it's gonna go, so they make it go how they know. Sell it to you like they saved the goddamn day. Aw, honey, 'course you don't feel so good after that. Trust me, this is just the start. You got a great little boy. It's all uphill from here. Or downhill. You know what I mean. I got four boys, I mentioned. All of 'em got boys of their own now. I got eight grandboys! I can't do nothin' but boys. And will you look at this beautiful boy you got! I know a lot about boys. Still hurting? Yeah, it's not always so comfortable right away. What's his name? Walker, huh? I like that. I like that a lot. That's a fine name. Well, you guys are looking just great. This looks all right. Feeling all right? It's gonna take a little getting used to. No doubt. For you and him, both. Practice, patience. No rush. You just take it easy, he'll do this thing, and you're gonna get to know each other just great, believe me.

It was like having Oprah at my bedside. My gratitude was quasi religious. *This* I could do. I could do this. I could right things this way. Bring on the oxytocin flood! Where else would I have learned? Who was going to teach me? What would have become of us on a different ward, instead of darling Donna, one of those demented can't-be-bothered formula-happy bitches? And me in my sorry stitched-up shock?

She came back before we were discharged, gave me her number.

I don't usually do this, but give me a shout if you need a little cheerleading, will ya? Been doing this a long time, now, so lay it on me, whatever problems you got. First few months apt to be a little rough, nothing to get too worked up about, just gotta get through. After that it's gravy. Fourth trimester, they call it; think of it like he's just not really ready to be on the outside yet. Nothing so easy once you get the hang, though. Nothing like a little boy. Nothing in the world like the way a little boy loves his mama. You the queen now, little mama.

His latch is shallow, I explain to Mina. *So you're engorged, which discourages your supply.*

My mother is sitting on the arm of the couch, listening intently.

Listen to the expert, she says.

And meanwhile it's painful, so you can't relax, which also stems the flow. Which means he's not getting what he needs to get stronger with the latch. So, vicious cycle.

Lookie-look at the La Leche League captain, my mother says. *You got yourselves a regular consciousness raising here. How vintage feminist of you.*

Zev's asleep, my milk still dribbling down his cheek.

He was hungry, I say, and Mina does the laugh-while-crying.

You think?

People like to pretend that small children and animals aren't sentient, so as to more easily perpetrate horrible crimes against them. It's easier that way, to isolate them or let them scream or eat them or ignore them or hit them or violate them, chain them to a bed. Pretend that what looks like relief or gratitude or love or calm or fear or outrage or pain is just a reflex, nothing more.

They sure do fill your arms up, these creatures. So good at being held. Then guilt washes ashore and I want Walker. I miss *my* baby, who's in some other room, in some other woman's arms.

Mina takes Zev back and I have no one. Which, you know, right, of course.

It was my friend Jess who gave me that Dylan bootleg, I recall. The newborn babe with wild wolves all around it. The highway of diamonds with nobody on it.

Mina wraps Zev up on her chest so her arms are free, then leans forward over the coffee table and eats a second helping of pasta with her free hand. Balances the bowl precariously on a knee, and scarfs it.

Paul refuses to come inside me.

It's okay, babe, I tell him. *Really, babe, it's okay.* I even go so far on occasion as *I want your hot cum deep inside me,* because who doesn't want to hear that?

But he refuses. He doesn't even get me a washcloth anymore. It would be nice for him to get me a washcloth. It's not that big a deal to get someone a washcloth.

He says he's not ready for another kid. Yeah, no shit, me neither. But I read that absorption of semen boosts serotonin in the female brain, so just call it a gesture of good faith: are we in this trench together or aren't we?

It's strange, that whole fallacy of "ready," because Paul is like over-the-moon obsessed crazy about Walker. I mean, it's ridiculous. I get stopped in restaurants so people can tell me how adorable Paul is with the kid. I find myself elbowing him out of the way so I can have a turn wiping the kid's ass once in a while. This is a pretty good problem to have, admittedly.

Usually it's the ladies you hear about getting so swirled up in being someone's MOMMY they cease keeping informed about international affairs and lose interest in blowjobs. Not so at our house! Fun with gender-role reversal, over here. I snapped at him yesterday to please, please stop singing "The Wheels on the Bus" for five minutes. Please just shut up with the fucking wheels on the fucking bus. Can we just drink our coffee in peace? Please ignore the baby for a minute and talk to me. The baby is fine. The baby is safe. The baby is happy. And I'm kind of terrifically lonely, over here. Maybe rub my neck? Maybe rub my feet? Maybe make me dinner, maybe make me laugh? Remember that cobalt hemp/silk flapper number I had on with the boots when we met for the first time in the hall before a faculty meeting? Remember how I caught you looking at me in the middle of that meeting? I could feel your attention on my thighs. And remember we had a whole silent conversation, both of us blushing, through that whole meeting? Remember how you tended not to stand right up against me in public because you'd get hard immediately?

Now it's all, *do you think another banana will constipate him* and *did you pack the wipes and an extra shirt and the bib* and *we can talk about it but honestly a little diluted juice once in a while seems like no biggie* and *where are the snacks* and *did you remember the thermos* and *I think the blue sweatshirt* and *it's too cold for no pants don't you think?*

Things start to get fuzzy around puberty, with hormones and trauma doing their muddy two-step on memory. Depression and memory loss the best of friends.

Lost in a private-school morass of Sarahs and Jennys and Melissas and Lindsays, hideous rich girls so brainwashed and servile they were destined to spend their lives whipped into a tooth-whitened nail-polish cardio bronzer plucked-and-waxed chemical-peel synthetic fertility-treatment hormone-replacement reproductive surgery froth.

In the wake of Bat Mitzvah season we sprouted simultaneous breasts and mustaches. Despaired our acne, the frizz of our hair. Rose at dawn to iron said hair with the commitment and resolve of conquistadores.

Those who had mothers were summarily carted to electrolysis and dermatology, put on meds for anything and everything as soon as possible: the Pill, months-long courses of antibiotics for acne, scorched-earth acne medication accompanied by detailed drawings of what your fetus would look like should you accidentally become pregnant thusly medicated, more Pill, antidepressants, more antidepressants.

My father did his damnedest not to notice my budding disfigurements: terrible skin, dark cheek fuzz, lopsided tits. As though failing to address these new and terrible disfigurements was the polite thing to do. So long as I was a kid I was of course his Pretty Little Princess; when shit started to go south he was like yeah, tough break, good luck with that, bye. The Blind Ophthalmologist Looks Away.

There were six girls named Lindsay in my grade alone. *Unibrow Lindsay,* we'd say to identify the particular, or *Fat Lindsay. Hand Job Lindsay. Bulimic Lindsay. Pretty Lindsay. Renfaire Lindsay.* Two of the Lindsays had the same last name, even. Lindsay Harris and Lindsay Harris. Unrelated.

No—we'd roll our eyes whilst talking shit—*the* other *Lindsay Harris.*

O Manhattan private school, where I learned to decode absolutely everything about a girl based on the smallest detail of grooming and attire. Upon graduation they might've offered diplomas in Object-Oriented Mysticism. I was forged in the fire of hell's lowest circle of Bitch.

That enraged cat noise we used to conjure female testiness, the claw. Girls whose mothers built them up and ripped them down. Girls with absent fathers, girls with doting fathers. Girls without mothers, sorry little lambs, primary wound glistening forevermore. Girls who hate each other with a passion because really they love each other. The ones who love each other up syrupy sweet because really they despise each other.

Girls who don't look at each other when they pass on the street. Girls who ignore the fact of each other whenever possible. No: who *pretend* to ignore the fact of each other.

My friend Shane and I decided to level with each other. Her wealthy ex-hippie underachiever "artist" parents were forever stoned; her older sister was fucking the wrestling-champ senior (fucking him constantly, fucking him everywhere). My mother was dead and no help regardless. So we had to be totally honest. Tell each other what the rest of the world saw. We occupied the same rung of the social ladder: Utterly Irrelevant. There was nothing to lose.

She went first: *No offense but your nose is suuuuuper Jewish. Your stomach is fat, I mean, like, weirdly way fatter than the rest of you. You have really good legs. And eyes. And okay, we seriously have to do something about your mustache. No offense. You could be almost pretty.*

No offense was Shane's thing. Offense: God forbid.

Then my turn: *Your face looks like an alien's. Your weird eye fold is creepy, and your eyes are so far apart, like practically on the sides of your head. It makes you kind of look like a fat fish. Let's just leave your body out of it for now. You wear really ugly clothes. No offense. Your hair is amazing, don't ever cut it. Maybe a deep conditioning once a week, though, because it's kind of dry. Let's wax your eyebrows.*

There was a moment of quiet where we each came to terms with the realities. Then we got busy. She helped me bleach my mustache with some stuff we stole out of her sister's vanity. It stank and stung.

We bought a home waxing kit at the drugstore, little plastic tub of brown wax you melted in a saucepan of boiling water. I accidentally gave her a tiny second-degree burn on her nose and took more off the left side, but she looked way, way better anyway.

We went on pretending to be friends through high school. She got good grades, went to a good college, became doting auntie to the legions of children sired by her sister and the wrestler. Looks like she's planning a wedding now, pretty into it. (*Cannot wait to be Mrs. Jason Fishman!!!!*) Professional engagement photos, assload of makeup. What the fucking hell has happened to her eyebrows? They're entirely gone, drawn on. Her poor eyebrows.

It was Arlene—my father's one-time high school girlfriend and blink-of-an-eye soul mate—who took pity on me and carted me to an electrolysis salon, the dermatologist, and her fancy-pants gynecologist, appalled I hadn't yet seen one.

Norman, I heard through the wall, *they're supposed to go when they start menstruating!*

Do you think she's, ah . . . do you think she is?

Norman, the trash in the bathroom reeks.

I didn't know, he told her.

I had been menstruating since just before my mother finally sailed off and away.

I'd gone around the corner to the drugstore alone, hands shaking, to get pads. There was a hospice nurse living with us. I'd wrap each pad, once used, in half a roll of toilet paper, stuff it way down into the trash can the nurse used for all the hospice detritus.

You didn't know!? Norm, she wears a double D.

I guess I . . . didn't know.

Arlene led me into a hushed, gray-toned waiting room on the bottom floor of a townhouse in the East Sixties and pinched my arm, leaned over, whispered *Jackie O goes here.* This was meant to be soothing, I guess.

Without much fanfare the good doctor introduced me to a speculum, mauled my tender lopsided titties, and hesitated for not even a second to put me on the Pill, citing "irregularity." A truly dumb-ass thing to do to a wonky motherless fourteen-year-old with big lopsided tits and a mustache, still years away from the faintest hint of possibility of sexual intercourse.

The good news, he told me, was that since I'd be on the Pill anyway I was eligible for the miraculous new acne medication! It worked wonders, he said, referring me to a dermatologist. Oh, but it was also "strongly recommended" that the acne medication be taken alongside an antidepressant, since it was known to cause/exacerbate "mild-to-severe" depression/psychosis. So not the best idea, because ever since the excellent ninth-grade English teacher had assigned us Muriel Rukeyser's "Effort at Speech Between Two People," the line "When I was fourteen I had dreams of suicide" had been replaying like a mental rosary I worked my way around. I rehearsed the ways I could do it. Pills, wrists, subway leap, roof leap, gun, noose, bridge leap, oven. Only our oven was electric and there were no guns anywhere I knew of.

Thusly medicated I gained forty pounds, never again

stood on a subway platform without the detailed flash of my body under a train, and have very little concrete memory of those years.

But my skin did clear right up.

There was Sweet Sixteen after Sweet Sixteen. Dresses from a store in the Village called Neo-Romantic. There were the uptight girls who acted all smart and detached, the mean, stupid ones who made everyone's lives hell. Girls with big ol' tits, their fates decided. Girls whose parents signed off on surgery to have said tits removed, replaced with appropriately demure ones.

I did have this one friend Rachel—an okay one, I thought: smart and ambitious and quirky and cute, with a big honking laugh—but by junior year she turned out to be yet another boring ano-fucking-rexic. Her doe eyes went bug over the course of the spring. Plain iceberg lettuce her big thing. Quirky interesting smarts starve-starve-starved away.

You're not having lunch? I would ask, chowing. Eating, and heartily, in public: my big protest. One-woman sit-in, private-school performance art: masticating food that I would then actually digest.

I already ate. You weren't supposed to say anything to the anorexics. It was considered rude.

Oh, really? What'd you eat?

She glared at me. Stupid cliché! Teachers didn't seem to care, her parents didn't seem to care, none of the other girls seemed to care, and in good time the admissions committee at Harvard didn't worry about it too much, either.

There were the teeny-tiny girls (always popular), big-boned early-to-develop girls (never popular), A-list girls and B-list girls and C-list girls and D-list girls. The B-list girls who got a new haircut and the accessory of the moment or landed a guy of note and suddenly found themselves catapulted to the top. The C-list girls who just banded together to create their own little utopia.

Those are the girls you want to be, it couldn't be clearer in hindsight. Early anarchists. Badasses. They didn't bother, exempted themselves, turned their backs and took up softball, computer science, gardening, poetry, sewing. Those are the ones with a shot at becoming fairly content happy/tough/certain/fulfilled/gray-haired grown women.

An important takeaway from those horrible, if hazy, years: whoever tries hardest is out. Too loud, too much makeup, fast talk? Detectable need? Fragility? Any indication of effort? Automatic out.

Disqualified.

Thank the good Lord almighty there was no Internet back then. Thank fucking Christ there was not yet Internet.

Why couldn't I just enjoy it? Why couldn't I be calm and at peace and fulfilled and engorged and certain and calm? Why did lack of sleep make me feel like I was going to die? And why then couldn't I simply hand the baby over to someone else and take a nap? And why, when he cried, when I had nursed and burped and hugged and kissed and changed and nursed and burped and changed again, when he kept crying, when the crying went on and he wouldn't sleep and the days unwound sunrise to sunset, when I hadn't eaten or changed clothes or bathed, when I had no one to talk to, no one to sit with, did I feel like putting him safely down in his crib and walking out into the park and sitting on a bench without my coat on until I died? Why so numb, so incapable, so enraged, so broken?

It's in your blood, my mother said, and laughed.

Rest for a while, Paul would say.

No, there would be no rest for me. There was no rest to be had. There was no escaping the brutal enormity of it: I had had a baby. I had been cut in half for no good reason, and no number of dissolving stitches was ever going to make me whole again. The hysterical imperative was to Feed Him from Myself continuously, no compromise. I had to be vigilant. Omnipresent. I had fallen victim to a commonplace violence, and now I had this baby and there was too much at stake. I had failed him out of the gate. Deprived him the vital, epic journey through the birth canal, my poor doped-up kitten. Poor helpless boy.

We found a grandma stand-in finally, hired her for a couple hours a week. She was kind, the mother of two grown girls. She did whatever I asked, obedient and efficient, but I didn't want to ask. I yearned to be told. I needed to be shown. Also she was not my mother. She politely left the room whenever I bared a breast. Made terrible small talk when all I wanted was quiet. And me sitting there so wrecked, unable to give a straight answer about the kind of detergent I prefer she use for a regular load.

Why so jittery, so jumpy, so on edge, so upset?

Paul tried. He couldn't figure out what was wrong. We had a beautiful, healthy baby, did we not?

He got up with the baby every single morning at dawn. *That* kind of man. Dawn after dawn. Every single morning, when it was still dark out and I couldn't move, could not leave the warm enclosure of bed, the safety of that metaphore, uterus.

But inevitably he'd have to go teach or go to the gym or something, and there was this way the sound of the door closing behind him would thud in my chest, leaving me alone with the baby, a dark dread panic rising. How *could* he?

Okay, monkey. Mommy's going to open the fridge now, everything's okay. Mommy's getting an apple. Yes, an apple's what we need. Then Mommy's going to sit down on the couch, okay, yes yes, nice and easy, sure, sure, no problem, hey little bug, no problem at all, all is well it's a Tuesday! I don't know what happens next. Precious baby. Okay. We'll figure out our next move. That's right. Okay, let's have some boobie, settle down there little fella, all will be revealed to us soon, oh yes, yes indeed, that's it, nice and easy, okay, okay, okay.

I'd be downright frantic by the time Paul came home. Panicked and relieved and guilty and downright frantic.

Thank God, I would say, my voice taut. He'd take the baby and soothe and coo and smile and nuzzle as I watched from across the room, feeling very strange, very outside, apart from them. On a loop: you'd be better off without me. I should disappear. You don't need me. I don't deserve you. You deserve a well-adjusted little woman who undergoes major unnecessary surgery without complaint. Gets on with things. Knows how to nap when her baby is napping. One of those itty-bitty compact little uncomplaining bitches who never even have to buy maternity clothes. Whose periods get lighter and easier as she ages. No body hair, no mood swings. A happy wife. A baby-food maker, a clothes mender.

You hate me. Admit it. You think I'm a terrible mother. You do. Admit it. Admit that you hate me.

I hate what you're going through.

Fuck you, Paul! I'm not stupid! I'm not dumb! Be real with me!

Baby, I don't think you're dumb.

Admit you think I'm a fucked-up headache.

Which is what my friend Subeena used to call "Being a Bad Girlfriend." As in: I really like this guy. I'm going to try and not be a bad girlfriend and see if it works out this time. We both got dumped a lot.

Paul encouraged me to get out of the house. We took a family field trip to the local bagel place, a terrible franchise. Walked there slowly and sat in silence eating bad bagels while the baby snoozed in the sling. I couldn't take my eyes off this ugly cherub calendar on the wall, looking at dates—December 8, 10, 12, 19—wondering when I'd finally have the guts to end my life, exit the only possible way, leave Paul to raise the beautiful boy in peace. I was dead weight, poison, disease.

Sounds about right, my mother said.

The bagel place was grim and cold, air-conditioned in the middle of December.

Chicken spaetzle, the girl at the counter kept telling people was the soup of the day. Her name tag read SISTER KATE. Her boss was Brother David. I imagined them a cult, the bad kind. But isn't any mildly cohesive, somewhat happy family a kind of cult? The good kind?

I found myself pleading with my mother one icy night.

Could you please, please be a little bit maternal for a few minutes?

I didn't know how I would make it through the next few hours. I feared I might not make it through the next few hours. Her face went momentarily soft.

Yes, darling, she said, and cocked her perfectly coiffed head.

There was still a small openness in my heart for her, it was true. A pinprick from which blood or love or whatever still flowed. She was part of me, after all. I was part of her. No matter what, it was true. She was in me. You can't disown what's yours, no matter how hard you try. What's yours is yours is yours.

Thank you, I mewed, dropped a tear, two.

She came closer, spoke softly.

Could you maybe just explain to me what that means?

I bring cupcakes from the co-op.

He's had, like, seven wet diapers and there's no pink. And he slept for seven hours last night. It's a miracle. Is this weird for you?

No. It's great. Is that *weird?*

I was lying awake last night thinking is this weird?

But it's not weird.

It's not weird at all.

The thing is women have always done this, just not since formula and advertising were invented.

Which came first, formula or advertising?

Advertising. I don't know.

I nurse while she pumps to encourage supply. She says something about it being difficult to get out when the weather's so shitty and I say something like yeah, winter's a shitty time to have a baby and she says something like it's always kind of a shitty time to have a baby though isn't it?

I hated the pump. Vile machine, real torture device, with

its awful rat-a-tat wheeze. Mina absently rocks the empty vibrating bouncy chair with her foot, sips from a clay mug, stares out the window at the icy dark.

The *rat-a-tat-rat-a-tat* starts to sound like *not-alone-not-alone-not-alone,* and then it becomes *I-don't-know-I-don't-know-I-don't know,* and soon it's *right-at-home-right-at-home-right-at-home.* Then *you-don't-know-you-don't-know-you-don't-know.*

Oh, I say. *By the way. I love Muriel Rukeyser. I forgot.*

Look what my sister sent, she says, almost three ounces bagged in the fridge, a really good sign, means she's producing nicely. She holds up a swath of fabric. Floral pink. She reads from the tag. *"Hooter Hider. To meet the needs of modern, active nursing moms." It's a burqa. This perfectly sums up my sister. And this.*

Another contraption, designed to fit over the seat of a supermarket cart. So your baby never has to touch a supermarket cart. To protect your baby from the evils of supermarket carts. She balls them both up and stuffs them behind the couch.

I'm fond of this baby, her baby, the swirls of his fine black hair, the weight of him against me, newborn smell. Our baby.

I had no idea how fucked up this was going to be, she says.

Tell me about it, I say.

Why doesn't anybody talk about this? I mean, how stupid do you have to be to worry about strangers seeing your tits in the wake of this?

Here's the problem: we are taught nothing.

How to sew, grow food, preserve food, build things, fix things, make fires, birth babies, care for babies, feed babies, move through time, grow old, die, grieve, change, sit still, be quiet. Still and quiet, endless Interneters, quiet, quiet, quiet.

How to be alone, how to shut up and be with ourselves for five minutes, how to listen, how to be still, how to mark and process passage, how to ritualize, bare feet in the earth. Basic knowledge in shocking disuse while we tap away at our devices. To call us monkeys is to insult monkeys. Birthing and care of newborn humans a specialty now, an area of expertise, hired out. Basic biological functions, ceded a generation or two or three ago and by now vanished as if the knowledge never existed in the first place. Like if breathing became specialized, or, no—like if shitting became specialized. Like if some corporation struck gold convincing us all that shitting is not necessary.

You need not labor over the toilet, ladies and gentlemen! It can be difficult, it can be painful, it can be slow, so much can go wrong. We'll free you of the whole business. Your body isn't doing as good a job removing its own waste as you might think. Let us do it right, let us do it for you! And oh, that opening is so small, while your waste matter can be quite sizable. Why put your body *through* that? Scores of people suffer from constipation and bowel diseases, both of which can now be eradicated! Try our simple shit removal, a must for modern folk on the go who need not be bothered by traditional, filthy human elimination! Let us make a tiny incision near your bowel to remove the contents on a daily basis. Sterile. State-of-the-art. Simple.

Leave the stinking excrement to the apes and savages. You're better than that, and besides, who needs the embarrassment? Now you can know exactly when and where your elimination will take place.

And very quickly, within a few generations, no one remembers how to take a simple dump anymore. No one knows that a silly magazine can help, that straining is ill advised, that herbs or Epsom salts or castor oil as a last resort can be a fine thing.

But, ah, well, the years are rolling by and it seems as though, er, perhaps, heh heh, there's some, ah, human error and shortsightedness involved in these "advances" after all. Also turns out—who knew?—there's actually considerable benefit to the normal contraction of the bowels, the body its own best caretaker, judge, healer.

Take it easy, now, they're gonna get around to doing a study eventually. Maybe someone's grandmother remembers taking a shit, the idea that your own body might actually be well equipped to dispose of its own waste. It's like a freak folk tale: foreign and fascinating.

Meanwhile, pay no mind to your scar, sucker.

Everyone's so "worried" about me all the time. I haven't really "bounced back," as Sheryl says.

Sometimes I'm with the baby and I think: you're my heart and my soul, and I would die for you.

Other times I think: tiny moron, leave me the fuck alone so I can slit my wrists in the bath and die in peace.

In the café where I never work on my dissertation is the woman I've seen at the co-op with her brand-new baby. We smile.

Do you ever feel like you're completely losing your mind?

Her smile fades.

It's okay if you do. It's perfectly normal.

Her roots are brown and gray, the rest is dyed red. She's probably doing that thing where you refuse to part with the first look you ever liked on yourself. When she was like twenty-three, she dyed it for the first time and never got over being that girl with the red hair, loved making those salon appointments, felt very on top of herself. Oh, but sweetheart, time has passed you by.

We're getting along fine, she says. Bitch, please: sell it someplace else.

How old is she? (Head-to-toe pink, so safe assumption.)

Five weeks. Glass bead. Bud in bud vase.

Did you have an okay time with the birth?

She actually flinches.

Here, I say, tearing a page from my mostly empty notebook. *Here's my number. If you ever need to talk or anything, call me. Women aren't supposed to do this alone.*

I'll make her a casserole, sure thing. Hold the baby so she can take a shower or a nap. Nurse her, if she wants.

She takes the folded paper.

Thanks.

What's her name?

Luka.

My name is Luka, I sing. Suzanne Vega.

We weren't really thinking of that.

After she's gone, I do some research. Ancient Roman lore about a heroic woman who saves her imprisoned father from starvation and death by nursing him in secret. Roman Charity, it's called. See also: Rubens, Caravaggio, Steinbeck. Precedent! Ask your grandmother's grandmother's grandmother's grandmother. The Arabic term for people who were nursed by the same woman, some approximation of "milk-brother," implies a stronger relationship than that of two people actually born to the same woman.

I write to Marianne. *Guess what? I'm the neighborhood wet nurse now! How fourth wave is that!?*

With her wedding over, Erica's shifted her focus to sheer terror of pregnancy. (As well she should! Cackle, cackle!) We visit on the device while I fold laundry. On her screen she watches herself talk to me, plays with her hair.

They're "trying," but four months have gone by and nothing is happening.

It's been a while, she says. *I'm getting kind of worried.*

A tiny green sock in need of a mate.

Come on. You have to know better than that. Don't you? You do know better than that, right?

So, what? You think I should just not have a kid?

I think you should relax and go about your life and be grateful for whatever you get, and hope you get a kid sooner or later one way or another and be fine if that's not what you get, too.

Oh, right, Ari, because you had a baby and now you're a Zen master.

Uh-huh.

Fuck you, she said.

Whatever.

I'm really not that excited about how fat I'm going to get, though. No offense. Can I ask you a question?

That was a question.

How did you know you were ready? We got one of those predictors? Where it tells you literally to, like, the minute when you're ovulating? But we totally chickened out. Watched TV and got take-out instead. She turns around to make sure she's alone, lowers her voice. *Okay, honestly? Steve couldn't get hard. Too much pressure, he said.*

It's weird when people talk about readiness. I so don't work that way. My brain has absolutely no sway over my heart. I'm never ready. There is no such thing as ready. There is only doing, despite.

Sooooo maybe you're not ready.

A pair of Paul's boxers are tangled up with my pajama pants.

So how did you decide to go for it?

I did nothing to prevent it. Then some time went by and it happened.

Teeny-tiny T-shirt.

I mean, like, how long? How much time?

I don't know. A year?

That tiny green sock's mate. When Erica and I were very little, she used to call herself CaCa.

Well, she said, *I made an appointment to get all checked out and get a referral. Just in case.*

A tiny orange sock. Of course, because if you could remotely afford medical assistance—or if medical assistance was covered by insurance—you were definitely supposed to need medical assistance.

Honey, I say. *Sweetie. That's a bad road. Please chill.*

Maybe I don't want to chill, she whines.

This deeply tragic couple from philosophy are apparently on round like seventeen of that shit. At Cam and Betsy's last year some of us were politely shaking our heads at their ordeal, and Crisp got all overheated.

Being for fertility medicine is like being for the death penalty, he said. *If it's* you *who's infertile, if it's* your *kid the maniac raped and murdered, of course you're all for it, that's just instinct. But maybe you shouldn't be at the wheel, hmmm? Given our most ideal collective spiritual goal of, what's it called again? Oh, right! Humility.*

Jerry touched his arm and Crisp shook him off. Something fierce passed between them.

Do you know that America is the only first-world country in which the fertility industry is not regulated? It's just about money, like everything else in this fucktard democracy. Customers. Salespeople. No ethical regulations, no profit caps.

The sad, divorced English department guy spoke up: *so if they taxed the crap out of people who can pay a hundred grand to make themselves a kid, you'd be okay with it?*

Yes, that would be a start. Entitled fucks.

Jerry spoke softly. *Little harsh, isn't that?*

No, love, I don't think so. Not at all.

What if we'd wanted kids ourselves, Jer asked.

You mean like our friends? Who've completely lost their minds? Like my sister, who has fucking cancer now thanks to that shit? I'd say: my darling, we don't get absolutely everything we want in this lifetime.

Betsy brought some dishes into the kitchen, didn't come back. The weak of heart drifted off to refill their wineglasses and discuss university politics.

If I call my father at home, Sheryl always picks up the other phone and listens in. If I call him at work, I don't have to talk to her. The receptionist puts me through.

Hi, my girl! What's up?

Benign and distracted as ever.

Not much, I say.

A flash: forceps clamped around my father's tender skull, the twist and pull of some cocky wartime OB. A cigarette dangling from the OB's lips. A snap somewhere along the side of my father's head, a series of pops somewhere deep inside, where courage lies. His mother drugged, listless, passive, moaning, sweating, abandoned, dead to herself. The baby removed and isolated.

How's our beautiful boy?

Fine, Daddy. Good.

Good! Good.

We set up camp at my house or hers. We listen to music. I like the music she likes. I want to know it all. The days feel wonderfully full. Walker's occupied and content. I begin to wonder if I need Nasreen's anymore.

I could have ten children like this, I say, meaning together, as a team. Sitting around, eating, talking, blankets on the floor. I mean, no fucking problem. We say *um-hmm I know oh my God totally right that's normal yeah.*

I nurse Zev. Instead of pumping, Mina has the bright idea to nurse Walker, who's so much bigger and stronger and of course a total expert, so why mess with the pump? Screw the pump.

I wasn't sure if he'd take to her. He looked at me first like, *huh?* Then he giggled maniacally, the funniest thing, looked back and forth between us giggling his ass off. Then he totally went for it.

I hold the fort while she goes to the bathroom; she holds the fort while I make lunch. We stretch, we breathe. Walker plays, shows me things, is chill, eats, sacks out. We rest.

We say *yes exactly poor thing* and *I know, I know that's the whole problem* and *really, well of course!* We order in food from the questionable Thai place, the only Thai place. We compose a harsh email to the celebrity midwife, who's based in the city, takes on way too many clients and half-asses it all up and down the Hudson. She still hasn't responded to Mina's original plea for help, hasn't so much as made an appointment for a postpartum checkup.

I can't believe I got an oblivious cunt of a home-birth midwife, Mina says. *I was sure the whole idea of home-birth midwife canceled out the whole idea of oblivious cunt.*

Zev's gained two pounds in a week.

Formula! the pediatrician says. *What'd I tell you? A lot of women just can't nurse. Do we have your updated insurance info?*

This is what women have done since time immemorial. We've rediscovered normal. No sitting home alone going quietly insane, thankyouverymuch.

This is my motherfucking dissertation.

If high school was girls named Lindsay, Jewish summer camp was girls named Yael.

Jewish summer camp. The words taste of strychnine even now. It made you wonder if, damn, what if that whole idea about the Jews being an inferior race was actually kind of true? It was all fucking and Zionism, straight up. Zionism and fucking. Almost a relief to go back to school in the fall, and that's saying a lot.

But! We have Jewish summer camp to thank for Jess. My lovely Jessica. Co-counselor. Teacher. Guide.

Boyfriend girls, we called the ones who early on found themselves a boy and clung to him steadfastly. Boring blanks. I always thought that'd be a good band name. The Boyfriend Girls. The Boring Blanks.

(*Yeah,* Mina says.)

If you were friends with a boring blank and she got a boyfriend, you no longer had any place or import. You were only ever a way station to a boy. Space filler. Audience for endless recaps of boy drama.

Jess was not a boring blank boyfriend girl.

Jess was Jewish summer camp liberation theologian. From the Boston suburbs. Older, about to be a college senior. She was hot and fearless. She hated that place even more than I did, but her parents had *met* at this particular Jewish summer camp a hundred and thirty years ago. The dining hall was named after her maternal grandfather.

It's pretty simple, she said. *If I appear to be doing the things they approve of, they pay my credit card bill and leave me alone.*

She gave me *The Beauty Myth,* played the first Ani DiFranco album over and over. We held hands. She had just spent her junior year in India and now had a wardrobe of simple, sumptuous cottons and silks, jewel tones, whites, lavenders, skies, silvers. Her posture was flawless. Never a bra. Stuck her tits way out proud. Never washed her long, shiny hair. I played with it. She rubbed my shoulders.

Cutie, she called me. *Sweets. Honey bear.* We touched a lot. I'd never had a friend I could touch before. What woman had ever touched me?

Jess did nothing to court her prettiness. Had no interest in being pretty. Everyone worshipped her. And she was *my* friend. Mine!

She had been with several guys already. At least one of them fairly damaging. She never said what, but something bad had happened. Or many bad things. An abortion, I realized one afternoon, but did not seek confirmation. She had secrets. There was a kind of power in that.

Anyway, she was off guys. She was done giving a shit about guys. She wanted to hear about my mother. She wanted to know about my father and his women. She wanted to know about private school, the Lindsays.

She told me about women's studies, the Guerrilla Girls, Jean Kilbourne.

This was new: a girl I wanted to *be*. I blatantly copied her. Aped her, top to bottom. Soon I was wearing straw sandals and kurtas, got my nose pierced, stopped washing my hair. She taught me about Sharon Olds, cowboy boots, jewelry as amulet. She gave me Susie Bright, Grace Paley, Emma Goldman. She gave me Sleater-Kinney. The neti pot. Yoga. She gave me palo santo from Peru. She gave me vegetarianism. She gave me Hula-Hoops. She gave me Ecstasy. We made tea with honey and lemon and cinnamon and fell asleep wrapped around each other. We sang "Both Hands" to our charges, a gang of hormonal-to-bursting twelve-year-old girls we otherwise ignored.

One night, I was beet red admitting I was a virgin and had never had an orgasm—*I mean, I don't* think *I have, but maybe I have, I don't know*—and she very patiently, slowly, and assuredly reached down her drawstring pants to show me what an orgasm was. Watching, I understood that I was fairly far from ever having had one.

On a trip into town one night just before the end of the summer we got matching tattoos. Both of us high. Acorns. My left shoulder, her right wrist. Because however far the winds might carry us, we were certainly of the same tree.

She was only two hours outside the city at college, and for a while we saw each other all the time. We met up and down the East Coast, went to shows, me so giddy, all disappeared into her. The way she stood up front, screamed her assent, threw her fists in the air, and emerged hoarse, with a tear-streaked face, swollen and satisfied. My idol. We ate at diners after like we hadn't eaten for a week.

You and your dyke music, Erica remarked once. I hadn't thought of them as dykes, my beloved Indigo Girls, my Michelle Shocked, Dar Williams, Shawn Colvin, Le Tigre, my Ani DiFranco. I just knew that at those shows I was whole and right. I was a person. I mattered. I was in fact *not* stupid or fat or ugly or lame; I was smart and valid and right and well. I had a fucking voice. The women at those shows weren't gussied up like geishas. They talked of art, life, politics. They felt entitled to feelings and opinions and rage and poetry and laughter and tears and bodies. There was dissent. Looking "cute" was low on the list. Practical shoes were high. It mattered only that one articulate oneself properly and loudly and the rest of the world could fuck itself. I was beautiful. I had style. Substance. I smoked. Drove too fast. We're all clichés. You learn who to be from your friends. Especially if you don't have any siblings.

Or a sibling with nothing to teach you, Mina says.

Jess joined the Peace Corps, went to Ecuador, fell in love with a German guy, lives in Berlin now. She apologizes once a year for being so bad at keeping in touch.

Can I please hear about it?

What, birth? Craziest experience of my life. I mean, acid, heroin, S & M: kid stuff. Adolescent bullshit. Playtime.

What, because of the pain?

The pain is incidental. Actually, no; the pain is the point. The pain gets your attention. When something is actually wrong there's fear attached to pain, which is what makes it horrible. Fear is horrible. Fear is the fucking worst thing in life. When something's com-

pletely as it should be, and when you trust that, there's no need for fear, so pain is . . . whatever. A fact. A thing. Pain in itself doesn't always warrant fear. Getting that straight is the game changer. Blew my fucking mind.

Go on.

It approached death. You go down into places it's hard to get at in life, you know? Extremity. And there's no safe word. No, like, "stop this train, I want to get off." It was like being turned inside out. It was like my skin came off. My soul left my body. Ego firebomb. I thought I was exploding. Like, literally: becoming a star. It was galactic. And it goes on in these waves, which are really rhythmic and crazy. This . . . I don't know . . . like fucked-up primal cosmic rhythm. And you're alone in it. Your whole life, your whole self, just obliterated. It's like when you try to lose your everyday consciousness? That's why people drink or compulsively exercise or get stoned or whatever else? Because it rules. But with this there's, you know, redemption, survival. The minute it's over, the pain is gone, and here is the literal fruit of your labor. The literal fruit of your labor! You can hold him in your arms, wrap him up and hold him tight and keep him safe. How amazing is that?

Huh, I say.

Her fingers travel up and down the length of Zev's leg. He's really alert. I always thought infants were just kind of out of it, but turns out, nope, when they're born regular, they're actually—oh, hi—quite present.

Because it's not like a construct the way S & M is, for example. An agreed-upon game. There's no one holding the other end of the rope, as it were. Or it's some force you'll never know. Like . . . life, death, outer limits. I don't know.

She puts one of his feet into her mouth and nibbles on it. He pumps his arms, concentrates so hard on her.

And what about the baby?

What about *the baby?*

I don't know, how does the baby figure in?

The baby is a reward. The baby is the prize. The baby's a gift. Waiting across . . . a . . . like . . . mythic crossing. I don't know. There's before and then there's after. Before is this entirely different thing, and after, the before is irrelevant. Death, rebirth.

The baby's an innocent. Clean slate.

Completely. Isn't that the thing? Clean slate, in your arms, and: go.

Yeah, I say. *That's exactly the thing.*

She's awesome, Paul. She's so great.

He nods.

She sounds cool.

I love her, Paul.

He wipes down the counters, straightens a pile of mail.

I mean, she's way more fucked up than me.

Than I.

What the fuck, Paul.

Another thing I needn't bother trying to explain. She's like a big old bell I can feel ringing in the best part of me. The vibrations go on and on, clear away the cobwebs, all the dense, cluttered junk, and it's like oh my god there's so much space in here, I had no idea there was so much room in me, what a pleasant place I turn out to be. Recognition. Reunion. A light on that's been out a long time.

I really like this one. I won't wreck this one. I'll take this one slow.

• • •

So start from the beginning. What happened in the beginning?

I called my friend Ilana, who agreed to doula for free while she was getting certified. Bryan was here. Bryan had been here for a few days. The midwife was driving up from Poughkeepsie, taking her sweet time. It went slow. Bryan was sleeping. There are those moments you realize holy shit I am all alone.

Were you scared?

I was serious. I was focused. I wasn't tense. Tense is the worst. You're not supposed to tense up. After a while Ilana shows up and Bryan thinks she's cute, so they're flirting and I'm, like, both of you go away. Couple hours went by. Contractions were chill, pretty chill, every few minutes, but I was totally present, just had to stop whatever I was doing, you know? It pulled me out of whatever I was doing. Cutting an apple, had to put down the knife and just give my full attention to the contraction. Perfectly doable. No biggie. Okay. Midwife continues to not show up. Contractions get more and more intense. Got so I couldn't do anything else—couldn't have a conversation, couldn't eat, couldn't do anything but manage. Get through them. Must've been, like, seven hours in at that point. Midwife finally gets here and checks me and goes upstairs to take a nap, because it can take hours and hours, but I don't know. I was kind of looking forward to her being with me. Bryan was in charge of music, and he kept putting on this fucking cerebral indie-rock nonsense, like, trying to impress Ilana. I was, like, fuck you, I need some good R & B, some blues. Something. And the minute some detached new indie-rock number came on, I'd be, like, turn that shit off, off, off.

About nine hours in, Ilana vibed kind of timid to me, like kind of beside the point. Bryan's not timid but Bryan aspires to exist in mainly virtual space. He could not handle it. He checked out. I didn't care. The midwife came and went. I remember at one point watch-

ing her eat a sandwich in the kitchen, thinking what the fuck, lady? I got down on the floor when a big one hit, and suddenly she's paying attention to me. It was so clarifying; it was like the most stupendous high. Everything was clear. There was no room whatsoever for bullshit.

Can I just—I mean, I'm sorry, but what if something went wrong?

Then we would have gone to the hospital.

You make it sound not scary.

I guess if it were scary, it'd be scary. I mean, if you're scared, then it's scary. Life is exactly as terrifying as you want it to be.

God, I'm such a failure.

The next part was something else entirely. There were no breaks. So it was continuous, really fast, waves one after the other with no break between: wave crash and the next one is already cresting. Total cacophony, overlapping, you know? So just this crazy storm taking its sweet time with me. Fucking relentless.

Like motherhood!

And I was, like, moaning and begging at that point, like, please, I need a break from this, but nope, no breaks. It's got you by the neck, and it's gonna drag you if you don't ride it. So you'd better climb on and deal.

I couldn't have done it.

Of course you could have done it.

I shrug. She is nearly scolding.

Of course you could have done it. You got sold some fucking bullshit. And listen, I mean, yeah, if a nice nurse had appeared at any time in there like "you ready for your spinal now?" I would have been, like, FUCK YES. I would have been, like, RIGHT FUCKING NOW, BITCH. It's not that I'm supersonic or I, like, "don't mind pain." She framed her face and batted her eyelashes. *I just knew that this is how I wanted it, and I knew what happens to women who don't protect themselves. So I made sure I wasn't in a position to get fucked over.*

It's not until someone actually looks you in the eye that you realize how infrequently anyone actually looks you in the eye.

You were raped, essentially.

Thank you, I say, and do my utmost not to look away.

For a few days a month I want to jump every man I see. Then I get bloated and the belly rounds. Then I want to shovel food into my face for a while, resort to sugar. Then I get suicidal. Truly hopeless, scary sad. Start to want my mother. Relate to her. I am her. She was me. And that's when I start to really loathe Paul. Can't stand the way he looks at me, speaks to me, touches me. Want away. Imagine setting myself on fire. Feel lied to, kept down. Am sure that when he's sweet to me he's faking it, doing his duty. That in his truest heart I am an inessential outline.

Today in the news: a story about a two-year-old Chinese girl abandoned to wander the streets of a large city. Surveillance cameras show her toddling into the street, where a white van hits and runs her over. The van stops very briefly, then moves on. For nine minutes the tiny girl lies bleeding and dying in the street while people pass by on foot and on bikes. The surveillance footage link warns EXTREMELY DISTURBING. I watch her toddling out in front of that van, see her struck, see her surprised small arms go up and out, almost like she's reaching for someone.

I can't stop seeing it. I light a candle and try not to throw up. All part of the cycle.

The rusty wheel keeps turning as if cranked by some invisible arthritic hand. Tomorrow or the next day or the day after that I'll bleed. And it'll be immediate, a lifted veil. All light and peace and the headlines won't destroy my day. Everything is, will be, has always been, okay.

Volumes upon volumes on exploration, war, violence, the life-threatening transformative journeys of man. But you can't talk about this. The fucking, the sadness, the dark, the blood, the light. They will burn you at the fucking stake for this shit.

In college there was the roommate with one fancy black bra she never washed. On scholarship, and *loathed* the rampant privilege. Which, yes, I got, and look, I'm really sorry, and please, I'm doing everything I can think of to live a life that's not about money.

She was so obsessed with money. The irony! I was hated for being rich, but I didn't *care about* money! *You're* the one who cares so much about money! So who's loathsome? Here, take my clothes. Here, let me get lunch. Sure, I'll spot you some. *I totally do not care.* Take some, take more. How much can I give you to prove I don't care about money? How much so you get that I'm not a greedy, selfish, walled-off princess? How tattered my boots, how cheap my T-shirts, how vintage my dresses? How many years wearing the same coat? How firmly steered in the direction of crappy café jobs and academia? It didn't matter. She had made up her mind to resent the shit out of me.

Then the roommate with a drug problem. She came and went like a ghost, barely hello, did not want to know me. Was fucking a guy in a band. Rarely around. Beautiful guy, terrible band. The guy hit on me occasionally.

Then there was Shira. Sweet slut from a religious family in Jersey. Her mother was dying. Fall of our sophomore year, starting a second round of chemo. Lymph infested.

Mine died when I was thirteen, I confessed over dosas one night. The dead mother game was old hat. I could be a friend to her.

Mine's going to be okay, she said. I froze mid-bite. She kept right on eating. Um, sure.

She was skinny with big tits. Completely obsessed with this very clean-cut guy who treated her like absolute shit. I still couldn't sell my virginity, much to my despair. She refused to speak in detail, but she'd display this coy little smirk whenever it came up, so I'd know they were fucking. I was supposed to envy her for fucking him. She was a kind of moron, but she had the sweetest gap-toothed grin.

Our friendship ended when I went home with her for Rosh Hashanah and her father turned out to be this vile fulfillment of every Semitic stereotype you've ever heard. I mean, the guy was like a Nazi cartoon made flesh: greasy, fat, balding, hook nose, sallow complexion, spit when he talked, black standard-issue yarmulke. Overpowering body odor. Sweat spots in the armholes of his food-stained cotton-poly button-down. It was like he was done up as Dirty Jew for the KKK Halloween party.

He went out of his way to welcome me, zeroed in.

Ariella. Grandchild of survivors, I hear.

Yup.

And somehow within about three minutes we arrived at how the Palestinians didn't deserve to live.

They're lucky we let them exist. It's charity.

Shira was helping her mother serve soup, back and forth

between the kitchen and the dining room. She made a sad face like, yeah, whatever, he's a little over-the-top.

It went on and on. He hit all the high notes.

We could wipe them out like nothing. We should. Israel has always belonged and will always belong to the Jewish people. The concerns of a filthy bunch of nomads are not our problem.

Excuse me, but that's, like, really racist.

Shira came back with the last of the soup. Everyone else at the table was eating or nodding or staring off into space.

They want us driven into the sea, and I suppose you think we should let that happen. In the interest of—what?—political correctness? Well, I'm sorry, little girl, but the survival of the Jewish people is paramount, and the fact remains. Hiding their weapons stockpiles in the midst of women and children so they can cry horror when the women and children get hit. I would happily round up every last one of those animals and gas them. Israel's economy is larger than all of its neighbors' combined! The highest ratio of university degrees to population in the world! Cell phones come from Israel. Modern fertility science. A tiny strip of desert turned into a blooming paradise, a light unto the nations. You can go live with the Arabs if you like, knuckles dragging on the ground, wear a veil, why don't you, and then come to my house and tell me what a worthy people they are.

You're a total jerk.

Shira switched rooms before winter break. Her mother died in the spring. After graduation the very attractive guy must have broken up with her for real because last I heard, she had married a pediatric dentist, made a bunch of kids, and lives in one of those upstate towns full of Orthodox Jews. It's probably not far from here.

• • •

Christmas Eve at Cam and Betsy's. The house is done up pretty festive, and everyone's in a good mood.

Cam and I do that thing where we both go in to kiss the right cheek, then both correct to the left, then very subtly freak out about how close we are to meeting at the mouth.

Aren't you, like, Jewish? I ask him.

So they tell me.

All righty, then. Merry Christmas.

Cat is dying for the scoop on Mina. She hasn't even paused to hate what I'm wearing.

I heard she had her baby.

Yeah.

She seems really cool.

She is.

Walker climbs into my lap. *Boobie,* he says. *Boobie?*

I let him nurse pretty much whenever he wants, and occasionally people ask in this airy voice *oh, are you still breastfeeding?*

Sure enough, condescending poli-sci guy's dead-eyed wife: *still breastfeeding, huh?*

Whoa, says condescending poli-sci guy. *If they're old enough to ask for it . . .*

In August at a café in Chatham, a second-home grandma type sat down at the next table and said, quite companionably, *you know you can breastfeed that kid until he's twenty, but you'll fuck him up for life.*

Oh, don't worry, I told her, just as companionably. *He's not mine.* Downright clairvoyant, wasn't I.

The look on her face! ("I don't argue where there's real disagreement," says the woman in my favorite Grace Paley story.)

Like they wish you would just stay home, out of sight. No, I will not stay out of sight. I will not go sit in the toilet in the middle of my dinner so you don't have to trouble yourself about the fact that you're a bipedal mammal, bitch.

I wish Crisp and Jerry were here.

Yes, I say. *It would appear that I am breastfeeding.*

Well, that's okay, Dead Eyes says.

Well, thank you.

Is it painful? Cat wants to know, ever the academic.

No. The comments are painful. The stares of disgust kind of hurt.

Who cares what anyone thinks? Paul says. A for effort, sweetheart.

My sister-in-law still nurses her kid, and he's, like, twelve, Cam says.

He's three! Betsy hollers.

Whatever, man, it's weird. He, like, massages her other one while she tries to carry on a conversation with you like nothing's happening.

Well my God, imagine, the nerve to multitask like that!

Everyone looks at me.

No, seriously, you should bury her up to her neck and throw rocks at her until she dies. What a crazy lunatic, offering her child a normal, healthy mammalian childhood. A woman in full bloom of health daring to use her body according to its biological design and function? Gross! When she could be purchasing from a multinational corporation a totally inferior product for the same purpose. That's downright un-American. And to do so within full view of an intellectual such as yourself!? Tie her up and SET HER ON FUCKING FIRE.

Paul is stock-still. Betsy emits a nervous, high-pitched giggle, and Cat keeps taking these extraordinarily small bites of her food, and I think: I fucking hate you. I really fucking hate you all.

Then, oh great, just wonderful, of course, sure, my mother is resting an elbow on the mantel, nodding at me, mock impressed.

The doctor told me breastfeeding was "for the natives," she says. *They had these pills you could take so you wouldn't make milk. The nurses were adamant about formula. I hardly saw you the first five days. It was absolute heaven.*

Before anyone says anything else I gather up the baby and go out the front door with a tit still hanging out.

Slam. I forgot my bag, which has my keys in it. I sit on our stoop for a while, heart pounding, tears a-rolling. Then I carry Walker down to Crisp and Jerry's and sit on *their* steps for a few, trying to calm down, waiting for something. Can't tell you what. A sign. Absolution. Grace. None shows, but when I knock, Mina opens up and I don't have to explain a goddamn thing. She locks the door behind us.

Weeds or flowers, Marianne told me the first time we had dinner. She singled me out early. I was terribly flattered. *Those are your options. Are you hardy, do you have that sturdy beauty? Or are you a delicate cultivation? Nothing sadder than a weed hard at work to become a flower. Or a flower pretending she's a weed.*

Isn't that kind of essentialist?

Weed or flower, sweetheart. Weed or flower.

On the last day, bleeding pretty much over, back to normal, I try to convince Paul it's okay. "Safe," as they say.

Please, I say as we near the end. He's on top, which despite the weight of history and religion is truly my favorite. Lately it feels like this is the only way I can get anywhere near him.

Baby, I say to him, *it's okay.*

You sure? He is unconvinced, but there is some willingness to be convinced.

Yes, baby, yes. Please. Yes.

You're sure?

The thought of him coming inside me, just this once—like old times!—is itself almost enough to push me over the edge. I'm close. So close.

Please, I beg him. *Please.*

The uterus is a monster. Insatiable. It wants to eat my brain alive. The minute I begin to relax and really inhale, exhale, clear my head, look around, start to see the world again, recognize myself and the people around me, at that very moment there's this malevolent whisper, this taunting *have another baby, have another one, c'mon, what're you, chicken or something, when are you going to have another one, go for it do it do it do it come on come on you know you want it you want it, you know you do.*

Before I had a baby it was all about are you going to have a baby? How many more years left until you can't have a baby? What happens if time runs out and you've failed to have a baby? Will you have a baby? Will you, will you? What if you miss out and *don't* have a baby? Tick tock, tick tock! (By the way, psssst! Don't you *want* a baby? Does it matter?? Have one!)

Fine, great, okay, so it all worked out and you had a baby before the iron curtain of forty-whatever came down, and you didn't even have to manufacture one out of questionable medical ethics, sheer will, and a suitcase of cash. High-five, you did it! Well done. Now: are you going to have another one? Don't you want another one? And another? Are you going to have another? Are you? Are you?? Having the one, it turned out, wasn't enough to get the world, or the world inside your body, off your back.

Paul finishes on my hip and I get myself a washcloth.

The final college roommate was Liz. Her father had killed himself. She was weirdly quiet and quite shitty at eye contact, sitting on a trash heap of anger, lying about it as hard as she possibly could. She was queen of the dykes, and I loved them all, my darling dykes, done with the defects of straight girls. It seemed to me at that point that one could not be a fully realized woman—nay, human—if one was not a lesbian. Or, distant second, a straight man. A person who is interested in women, in other words. A lover of women. A person for whom women are the focal point, the main intrigue.

I never had the cliché fag sidekick, dish about shopping and boys. Screw that. I had arrived at an understanding that straight women and gay men were uninteresting. Anyone interested in sex with men, no thanks.

Lesbians and straight dudes: so straightforward. It was all on the table. (Also they wanted to fuck me.)

I could not seem to be able to have sex with a girl, though; that was the only problem. I loved women, and loved women who loved women, but I remained stubbornly, fundamentally interested in the idea of dick. I liked being naked with women. Liked putting my mouth on girl skin. But I couldn't get the love palsy with a woman. A few tried to convince me I was just not ready to admit the truth. That I should run headlong into the particular discomfort a woman provided. Much confusion.

Important lessons were learned, however. Stand up straight, stop smiling all the time, stop trying to make everyone like you. Call it feminist. Call it whatever you want. Relax your face. Don't be so friendly and agreeable all the time, don't put yourself last, worried about everyone else's feelings first.

Liz and I criticized each other constantly and immediately after graduation had the most insane hate-fuck of all time, after which we happily never spoke again.

Pricing and stocking dairy at the co-op.

Walker's at Nasreen's. I can't stop looking at pictures from last year on my device. I can't deal with the child as he is today; I've just barely wrapped my head around the child as he was months ago. In a year I'll be looking at pictures of him now, getting teary, wondering where the time went.

Back to work, deadbeat, Naomi tells me. *You coming to New Year's Eve? Gonna be amazing.*

What happened when the band broke up?

I played with a few other bands for a while. Sort of for hire, but none of them worked out. Energy wasn't right. Not like the energy was right with Kelly and Stef and me either, though. At all. Stef was the worst. Most insecure girl you've ever met. Determined to make everyone else feel as bad as she did at all times.

Yeah, you can kind of tell.

Kelly was great, but so, so depressed. She just withdrew and withdrew. There was nothing anyone could do. The harder I tried, the more gone she was. She had her drug friends, and they had this, like, private language. She was already long gone when she died. It was kind of anticlimactic.

Yeah, so it's not even exactly sad.

It's just kind of this relief.

But you can't explain that to people.

No. The sadness is kind of just incidental.

What's this about Stef becoming a born-again Christian and starting some sort of Christian rock camp—is that true? And there's a documentary about it?

Rocking Out: Badass Like Jesus.

So then what?

I did nothing for a long time. Fucked men who required my full attention, lived weird places, whatever. OD'd. Spent some time in the hospital. Wrote. Traveled a bunch. Just took off, no place to come back to.

Where?

Rome for a while. Frankfurt. After the worst and final guy. Maine. New Mexico. An artists' colony in Wyoming for two months out of every year. Life feels really full when you never stop moving. Until it doesn't.

What was the hospital like?

Are you asking about ECT? It was not like in One Flew Over the Cuckoo's Nest. *Once was plenty. I don't remember a lot of it.*

Abruptly she picks up her device.

No one calls me anymore.

No one calls anybody anymore, I don't think.

Six A.M. Walker's howling. I get him, let Paul sleep in.

Thank you, babe, he says from under the pillow.

Kitchen. Make oatmeal, fill the sippy. Assist with spoon. Invent a game with blocks, which buys me about six minutes of peace. When he tires of the blocks, he toddles over to me and buries his face in my leg, shrieks with joy, blows a raspberry, laughs his ass off.

Boobie? Boobie?

I'm not saying it happens every minute of every day, and I'm not saying it renders the other stuff unimportant, but there are moments of the most crazy all-encompassing joy. What a phenomenally beautiful kid. A funny, dear child. Kind and open and loving. *Love bug,* I call him. *Monkey. Shmoopee-doo.* If the world interferes with him, with what is loving and open and funny in him, I will rear up in full roar. I will break the world's neck with a swipe of my mighty paw, no warning. Anything fucks with this kid, I will fucking kill it.

It's the wildest thing: I really and truly love him more every day. I had no idea. You supposedly fall in love with them the moment they exit your body, but in the aftermath I was just like WHAT THE FUCK WAS THAT. And I have to believe he was just as much like "what the fuck" as was I. And there we both were. The relationship develops, the getting to know each other. I mean, he's completely and totally dependent, which is very intense, but it's not love. Over time I have to let go of him. That's love. That's the work.

But what if *I* fuck with this kid? What if *I* interfere with what is loving and open and funny in him??

We watched a movie last night, me and Paul. One of those wacky road comedies in which a box of human cremains figures prominently. At the end, the devastated/hilarious widow scatters said cremains off a seaside cliff and winds up, thanks to the wind, covered in most of it herself. Whenever you see cremains used in the plotting of a comedy, you can be sure that no one involved knows anything whatsoever about death.

Paul could not understand what it was in that dumb-ass movie that I objected to. Sometimes I get lonely in my darkness. Marriage is tough. You have to try and be your best self at all times. The horrid, petty, lying sack of shit you know in yourself has to be daily wrestled to the ground. And it's not like your heart curls up and dies; it continues to want and want and want. It, too, must be wrestled to the ground.

As soon as we turned off the movie we could hear a bat in the eaves. *Me me me me me. Me me me me.*

When he was asleep I masturbated to a guy I loved for a few weeks once, our whole relationship naked in my apartment. I remember him in perfect detail. It never would have worked out between us but Oh My God.

The bats kept it up all night. *Meemeemeemeemee.*

This house is a nineteenth-century mansion; I forget to see it sometimes. I sit in the living room and marvel. Vast space we're growing to fill. I wonder if we'll have another baby. So ripped apart. Like thrill seekers must feel when they jump out of planes. Broke me. Killed off the old self pretty thoroughly. That other woman is gone. That girl.

I think I expected to feel like Walker was some extension of ME, a little piece of ME. It's not like that at all.

you know she had the baby in your whirlpool, right?

yeah she warned us. jer got all misty about it.

Cat wonders what I'm up to, wants to hang. I don't need her anymore. I have a real friend now!

Little under the weather, I lie. *Plague of day care.*

Bat in the house, I text Will.

Nothing you can do about it but chase them out with a broom. Usually they show up in the fall, but it's been so

warm the last few days, maybe it woke up confused. They say the next global pandemic will almost certainly come from a batborne pathogen.

Wonderful. Thanks.

New Year's Eve.

Bryan's back.

some party in troy . . . he chimes. **wanna go?**

Fo sho, I reply, but autocorrect turns it into **Go who.**

New Year's isn't Paul's "thing." I used to fight him on it, force festivity, but after a few years of winding up in tears while the rest of the world kisses and hugs and shouts and dances and sings, I decided to disregard him entirely, cranky old man. So far, so good.

I direct Bryan to Crisp's top-shelf if stale ecstasy, which is in an industrial-sized pill bottle labeled Wellbutrin, over which there's a purple permanent-marker happy face.

Gonna sit this one out, kids, Mina says.

I take spontaneous pity and text Cat. She is dressed and on her stoop to meet us twenty minutes later.

This is Bryan, I tell her.

Hey.

Hey, back.

The night is pure ice. Naomi's savings bank is adorable, just me and Bryan and Cat and a few hundred Utrecht and Bennington and Bard and Vassar and Skidmore students dressed up like me in the ninth grade. Combat boots, Jessica McClintock dresses, glasses, the works.

Cat's displeased with the crowd. She sets about getting us drinks like she's on a cheesy scripted CIA drama. She is too cool for school. I don't even want a drink.

She does not fuck around, Bryan observes.

Indeed she does not.

I dance a little, slowly, takes time to get into it. Bryan dives right in with some self-conscious robot moves.

Lights turned off for maximum relief, Naomi's invites say at the bottom.

Just because they cut that kid out of me doesn't mean my hips are good for nothing. I can still swing them okay. I'm not dead yet.

Bryan's game. We're getting into a bona fide groove when Cat returns.

You don't have to be stoned or psychic to see that Cat is plainly shit-her-pants terrified of dancing. She just stands there holding three beers. She hands them to me and scurries off to find a bathroom. I hand one to Bryan and two to a passing undergraduate in fishnets.

Cheers, Fishnet screams, keeps moving.

I've never actually laid eyes on your husband, Bryan yells.

I've never actually laid eyes on your cock, I yell back.

What's the deal with you?

The deal?

Are you happy?

Am I "happy"?

Yeah. Happy.

Shrug. Let's puzzle that one out, shall we? Happiness.

I dunno.

Is there someone else who would know?

Point taken.

There is the most adorable girl nearby, six feet tall with short hair, like nineteen. In love with herself, dancing. I study her, and begin to copy her.

How do you feel?

High!

Aside from that!

How does one know how one feels?

One feels and then observes one's feelings.

What if one doesn't know how one feels? What if one has no fucking idea what feeling is even fucking supposed to feel like?

Then one might not be happy.

I stop dancing, hold out my hand for his beer, and suck on it. Fresh, sweaty flesh moves all around us. They are so lovely, these girls. When the time comes I hope they will avail themselves of all the biological-feminist childbirth literature they can get their capable hands on. May they attend one another's births in full bloom. I hope they worship the moon in sisterhood. Bryan is staring at me.

Do you think your husband's happy?

Probably not. I lean in real close so I don't have to yell. *I'm kind of a bitch.*

His smirk is the most genuine thing about him, the cutest. This is a terrible sign in a person, and most irresistible. Or used to be.

You're beautiful, he said. *You know that.*

My response to that kind of thing has always been mortified disbelief and a pathetically thrilled *shut the fuck up.* But I let it stand. Who is he to me? Maybe I am beautiful. Maybe the scant light is hitting me right, maybe my hair is falling nicely. Maybe my shirt is draping well, maybe my ass angles high and round. Maybe some hint of lipstick still remains. Sure, that's right: beautiful.

It's a stupid dare, Bryan's stare. Cat's back and he's still looking at me, but I'm out. Bye, little boy. I am a grown-ass woman. Faced down death and lived to tell the sorry shocked stitched-up tale, and here is an overgrown boy standing here trying to use me for some game. Who am I to him?

I disappear into the crowd, lose myself in all the sweaty young.

Omigod! Naomi almost tackles me. *You came!*

On the car ride home Cat is in the front seat positively purring. Bryan has his hand on her thigh, and now that we're out of the party she's jumping around to the music from the radio. She's been liberated. Maybe she got high. She is not herself. I'm stretched out in the back, still sweaty from all that dancing. I danced hard. Everything is dreamy.

Donut drive-through, Bryan points out.

Omigod should we? SHOULD WE!? Cat is out of her mind, and I kind of like her this way.

New Year's Day. I make dinner for Mina and Bryan. Paul goes to the gym.

He's good people, Mina tells me.

I know, I say, sounding defeated.

We have good chocolate and hot buttered rum and lentil stew, not in that order. We have a stack of recent tabloids, a vaporizer, Bryan as acting DJ, and two sleeping babies. We have a fire in the fireplace. Other than Bryan's constant photographing and posting of everything, it's nice.

I'm going to barf, Mina says. She throws her tabloid at me. Cover story about a celebrity hospitalized after her fourth C-section in five years. All those incisions. Uterus covered in scar tissue. Placenta had nowhere to attach.

Don't blame the victim, I say.

Cool, let's be victims and no one can ever blame us for anything.

Maybe you should try to, like, really stigmatize surgical birth, Bryan says. *Like a guerilla PR campaign about how weird and dangerous it is to have your baby surgically removed. That's good stuff,* he says, reaching for his machine.

You know why I hate women?

No, doll, tell us, Bryan says to me. *Why do you hate women?*

Because they didn't prepare me. Because they didn't help me. Because they let me do this alone. Because they avoided knowing, mostly, themselves. How could they let me fall down this rabbit hole? They knew what was going to happen. Every woman who's ever lived is supposed to know.

Thank goodness we don't have daughters, Mina says.

Thank fucking God we don't have daughters, I agree.

Sheryl told me she played cards in labor. Reported it without affect. Beep went the machines. Beep beep beep. *And I said, oh look I must be having a contraction.* She giggled when she said it, like she was talking about someone else's body, someone else's birth.

Maybe having given birth, you don't have to fear death anymore, Mina says.

Bryan is typing. My mother leans over and squints at his screen, her arms crossed.

We're as fearful of childbirth as we are of death, I say. *Why else do we do everything to try and numb and control it? Why else does no one like to talk about it? Everyone's scared. They're so scared they don't even understand they're scared, that everything's about fear.*

That's good, Bryan says. *"Everyone's so scared they don't understand they're scared."*

My mother rolls her eyes.

People have always feared childbirth, she says. *And people have always feared death. Since always and forever. There's nothing new under the sun.*

The local NPR affiliate is replaying some *Gifts of the Magi* special. *Think only of what you have,* booms a beautifully deep and frayed male voice, *and give no thought to what you lack.*

Hey, Bryan says later, before I go up to bed. Mina is passed out on the couch, Zev on her chest. The fire embers are still crackling. *Level with me here. Do you think she's, like, depressed?*

Uh . . . yeah.

Do you think she's, like, okay? Because I said I'd come back, but I can't stay forever.

I think it's not normal to have a baby and be by yourself.

She's not by herself. She has you! What am I supposed to do!?

You're supposed to hang with her. You're supposed to marvel at how nuts it is. Be indulgent. It takes time. That's it. Keep her company. Feed her.

I am *indulgent. All I* do *is support her. Yesterday she starts in crying out of nowhere, tells me she's exhausted and she needs to find a humane way to kill them both. It's bananas. And I don't know if this whole thing*—he grabs his own tit as if to offer it to me—*is really helping. Why not give the kid some formula and get on with it.*

That's not what she wants.

She's lost her mind.

She's not the first.

Are you some kind of witch?

Yup, I reply, and stare him down.

3

JANUARY

Waddling through the final days of pregnancy, exhorted to take long walks, I stumbled upon the Utrecht Historical Society Archive, which is a warehouse next door to the Utrecht Architectural Parts Archive, which is an even bigger warehouse, where you can find all manner of the most incredible old doors and windows and decorative ironwork and stained glass and lighting fixtures and clawfoot tubs and plumbing accessories and mantels and fireplaces and radiators and spindles, stair rails, newel posts, moldings, woodwork, and flooring. The kind of place where sensitive grad students imagine the quirky antiheroes of their dreams hang out. In a dusty pile of old periodicals I found a guide to breastfeeding, circa 1941.

Nurse your baby for one minute on the first day. Then nurse your child for two minutes on the second day, and three on the third, moving in this way toward fifteen minutes by two weeks, which is the most time your child should ever be at the breast. Crying is good for their lung development.

I paid five cents for it and waddled on.

Bryan is watching me nurse Zev. Mina is taking a nap.

Does Paul suck on your tits?

If I say yes, I'm kinky and disloyal, but if I say no, I'm a prude.

Do you want to suck on my tits?

Sure!

Sorry.

Come on. You have the prettiest little nipples.

I bare them at him, pleased.

Jew nips. The most delicious.

I sing a soft Misogynists refrain to baby Zev, who's got all kinds of fascinating new expressions: *not shy and won't apologize.*

It's fantastic, these babies and my boobs.

People don't want to hear about that, don't want to entertain it. Vast numbers will watch two naked girls online shit in a cup then eat it, but babies enjoying the living hell out of breasts as supreme source of endless free nourishment and good health for all remains taboo. Explain that to me in a way that does not skirt the historical imperative of misogyny. Go ahead. Try.

I'm good at this. Look at me, nursing two babies in tandem. I'm a damn fine nurse. I am way more than enough. I am everything. Give me a third. Give me a fourth. I am a font. Plenty to go around. Let me sit here, life all around me, in me, through me, down the front of my oversized shirt, forever and ever, amen.

Mina comes in, groggy.

Did you just nurse him?

Yeah.

But now I'm ready.

So nurse Walker.

Okay. She seems a little miffed. Which in turn makes me kind of miffed.

I turn back to Bryan.

So.

Yeah.

Are you going to tell us what happened with you and Cat on New Year's?

It's not very exciting.

I'll be the judge of that.

She was not at all into hurting me and could not for the life of her articulate anything interesting she might want me to do to her. And she kept, like, gazing at me trying to make out, and I was like, no, listen, I want you to squeeze my balls until I puke.

You should write a story about a world in which everyone has to have a baby, I tell him suddenly.

Like, it's enforced?

Yeah, I say. *Think of all the crazy shit people would do.*

No crazier than the crazy shit people already do, probably, Mina says. *Anyway, you can't tell a writer what to write.*

Sheryl suggests I come down to the city for a "day of fun." Paul's all for it. Practically pushes me out the door.

Baby, go. We'll be fine.

Sheryl wants to get our nails done. She's consumed with the idea that we get our nails done. I don't want to get my nails done. It smells like toxic death in there.

Oh lighten up, Ari, for God's sake. What do you *want to do, then?*

I can't think of anything. Or, rather, I can't narrow it down. I want an empty five-hundred-square-foot studio in Chelsea with someone else's name on the buzzer. I want to sit by a window in a café with a book and a pen while it rains. I want to take the train uptown to see someone at a party. I want to wear a hat without looking ridiculous. I want to get stoned and try on sumptuous clothes at boutiques. I want to spend an hour at a good secondhand store in Brooklyn. I want to wear something gorgeous and singular to a museum, and meet up with a bad-news lover. Toward the end of dinner (appetizers and a lot of wine) I want him to put his hand lightly on my breast until I begin to get feverish and we have to get out of there immediately, right now, pay, let's just go, it's okay that's a huge tip it's okay who cares c'mon let's go. I want to wake up the next day at noon in the beautiful light of his uncluttered space, kiss him goodbye, promise to see him again soon, maybe mean it. I want to go for a walk, to the farmers' market, sit all afternoon again with a strong latte and again a book, again a pen, aftershocks from last night's rash of orgasms. I want to see a movie with a girlfriend, talk about what we're working on, what we're trying to accomplish, what we're thinking. I want to laugh. I want a little house in the Catskills where I can lay a futon, burn some sage, shave my head like a penitent, spend my days reading and napping and writing and stretching and cooking in silence. Almost certainly I chose the nunnery in a former life.

So we go get our nails done, Sheryl and I, and then I don't recognize my hands with their dumb little squares of perfect.

Late afternoon I have coffee with Marianne. She eyes my manicure.

She'd recommended Chodorow's *The Reproduction of Mothering*; I'd found it to be a crock of shit. I talk Susun Weed and Ina May Gaskin and Maya Tiwari and Pema Chödrön.

Please not all that earth mother goddess shit, Ari.

Actually yeah all that earth mother goddess shit, Mari. Actually quite yeah.

I sit up straighter. Those are the feminist writers I consider important now. Feminism without focus on the body, the soul, the relationship between the two—biologically female bodies with distinctly female struggles—is of no interest to me. The body is the soul's home and expression. The body is everything. To harm the female body is the original and only crime.

Her brows are raised so high, they look spring-loaded for escape. You have to be careful about how you tense your face, because however you tense your face is what your face slowly but surely becomes.

I don't know about the wet-nursing as political act, Ari.

Well, hon, that might be kind of a massive failure of imagination on your part.

Her smile is both faint and rigid. I want to throttle her.

All right. She shrugs. *Prove me wrong.*

She glances at photos of Walker on my device. Bored smile. Lights another cigarette.

He's very sweet.

You know what's truly ridiculous? I had this idea that she'd be proud of Walker, that she'd love him because he is mine. That she'd want to mother him, too. That this new family would include her.

We part on the corner of Bleecker and Charles.

Be happy, Ari, she says.

Then I run thirty blocks up Seventh Avenue to catch the train, my boobs full and hard and aching. I thought I could be gone the whole day from my nurselings. Wrong. Okay, body, got it, read you loud and clear. Abundantly.

So, Bryan says. *Here's the pitch. The year is 2115. Humanity has lost the ability to lactate. The government controls all baby formula, and it's made under secretive circumstances, with, we suspect, mind-control additives. So babies won't grow up to question authority or think independently. Only one woman can still breastfeed. She is an ignorant farm girl from a poisoned American backwater. The knowledge was passed down by her mother, and her mother's mother, all the way back through a line of women who operated on pluck and principle back when these things were hotly debated or whatever. The government cannot allow this girl to nurse her babies, or anyone else's babies. She is a threat to national security, not to mention massive corporate interests.*

One and the same, Mina interjects.

If she shares her knowledge with other women, there could within a generation rise up a rebel army to overturn the status quo. So they dispatch an assassin, and the farm girl, with her cohort, goes on the run.

He looks up at us with a grin.

Yes, I say.

He does have good ideas sometimes. He just fails to follow through.

He frowns at her.

No, listen, she says, *the problem is no one cares about babies. I mean, they care about babies like "oh look at the cute baby" or "oh, ha ha, funny-looking baby with an old-man voice-over," but no one actually cares about babies. I mean, the details. It's boring. If I may.* She gestures at the strewn coffee table. *Breast pumps, lecithin, nipple blisters, fenugreek, highchairs. I mean, who cares? I don't even care.*

Ask her who the father is, Bryan says to me.

I don't dare.

Virgin birth, she says.

That's all she'll say.

Check this out, she tells me. Footage of Kristin Hersh giving an interview in Denmark while breastfeeding her one-year-old.

All you bitches are the same, Bryan says.

We look at him. One entity, her and me. One body. Boundaries are nothing but a refusal of life and love.

Oh I'm sorry; all you ladies *are the same.*

Better.

You agonize about wanting a baby not wanting a baby ambivalence about having a baby oh-time-is-running-out-and-I-want-a-baby and then you get a baby and you're all fucked up about having a baby. I mean, you wanted a baby, you got a baby, chill out and enjoy the baby.

Do you think, Mina wonders, *it might be a little more complicated than that?*

I don't know, people have only been having babies since, like, the start of time? Man up, ladies.

We're dumb cunts, I explain.

You are. You are dumb cunts.

Dude, believe me.

You guys, oh my God, check it out. She squeezes her right one, milks herself, sprays a foot in the air.

We clap and hoot and high-five.

• • •

At the co-op I have a new shift-mate. She's recently a grandmother and has just returned from ten days in Oregon with her daughter and new granddaughter.

Wow, I say. *Your daughter's so lucky to have you.*

Yeah, she says. *She was really grateful.*

Ten days, imagine that. Cooking, cleaning, laundry, getting up with the baby in the middle of the night. Saying okay, everything's gonna be all right.

I'm shelving the fair-trade dark chocolate; new gram is working on the gourmet peanut brittle display. I break up a bar of the fair trade and put out samples.

This chocolate, she says. *The best!*

Amazing, I agree.

Hard to go without every now and again.

What is it with women and chocolate?

I don't know that it's a woman thing, per se, she says.

O-ho, the second-wave police are out. Heaven forbid it might be true that female bodies are different. Heaven forbid we admit that living in these female bodies is different. More terrible and more wonderful. Because, what? We might lose the vote? Because we might get veiled, imprisoned? Best deny it, deny it, make it to the Oval Office, win, win, win.

Oh, it's most definitely a woman thing, I say, then turn my back and work in silence for the remainder of the shift.

Naturally you'll want to know how my grandmother survived.

My mother's mother. Tormenter of my tormenter. I have all her letters. Sure you're curious about how she got from Auschwitz all the way up to Park Avenue, to Westchester, to pay cash for the grand piano and the grandfather clock and bone china and the apartment and the house in which it all grew dusty. Exactly what primal torments did she endure and escape? Everyone always wants to know. They ask around it.

But you can't un-know, okay?

She survived by sucking Nazi cock. Nineteen years old. Survived with her mouth full of throbbing Nazi sausage.

All righty?

I found letters from after the war at the bottom of my mother's jewelry box.

She survived under a thorough coating of Nazi cum. Survived letting Nazis fuck her up the ass. Did you think these activities were new?

That's how she survived. It wasn't put exactly that way in the letters, but I got the message loud and clear.

Shocked? Appalled? Aroused? Please don't act all upset. You think she survived because she believed in the triumph of the human spirit? Because of faith, hope, Transcendental Meditation?

Please.

She survived by giving herself over to all things you like to look at on the Internet. You. Spare me the histrionics and go erase your browser history.

All the things they wanted to do to her and all the things they wanted to watch one another do to her. She survived by fully accepting it. Fucked in every possible way, by every possible combination of them. For three years.

Now you know.

One time I fucked two guys. I kind of liked it, but soon after felt awful, and the awful feeling was itself like an exciting evil drug I wanted more of. There was great freedom in being an object. Letting them use me, my body a thing to be used. The feeling was vaguely superior. Not even vaguely, come to think of it. Like I had transcended my soul, left the troublesome thing behind once and for all, no need for it. Bothersome thing.

The Nazis weren't all bad to her. A few were sort of sweet. Some went slow. One was a virgin. He cried, she said. Buried his head in her shoulder and wept like a child.

She got food, heat, a cot. The privilege of washing herself and her clothes. She didn't freeze or starve or get typhus.

Okay? That's how. Survival ain't pretty. Bookish and musical country girl, her butcher father's pride and joy, maiden no more. Beloved eldest, caretaker of the little ones. She had dreamt of attending conservatory in the big city where artists roam. Raped under the smoke, in the good old days before anyone had a cell phone with which to take pictures for the news outlets. Not that the news outlets cared. Her younger brothers and sisters weren't half so lucky.

Scene: Deportation. Death camp. Cold. Fear.

They get herded off the train into line. At the front of the line an officer sends most to the right and a very few to the left. My grandmother clings to her childhood friend Elsa. She's already been separated from her younger siblings. They reach the front of the line. The officer looks them over. They are huddled together trying not to cry.

Who made that dress, he barks at Elsa, who is wearing a gorgeous high-waisted wool blend with double seams and elaborate neckline with folds like flower petals. She was a masterful dressmaker from a long lineage.

She looks that officer square in the face.

I did, she says. Her German is flawless.

You did?

Yes. That's what I do.

You made that dress?

Yes.

You make dresses?

Yes.

To the left!

He appraises my grandmother next. A beauty, pale skin, bright eyes, nice tits.

Both of you! To the left.

A great story. There was going to be a movie about it, once. Two girls, best friends from girlhood, having lost their families, are saved by beauty and skill and friendship.

Well, Elsa worked her fingers to the bone creating fine garments for Nazi wives and children; my grandmother sucked cock. The movie people wanted to whitewash a bit. The screenwriter made it so that my grandmother was simply the romantic interest of a particular, tenderhearted Nazi officer. A love story, essentially. This infuriated my mother to such a degree that she nixed the entire thing.

They went ahead and made the movie about just Elsa anyway. There were Oscar nominations. A very stirring score.

You had to hand it to my mother.

Elsa lived to be forever and a half years old on a lake in Michigan with her voluminous family. Proud Survivor matriarch, classic breed.

The other whores showed my grandmother the way. Véronique from Paris and Helge from Berlin. They showed her how to hide a small part of herself. Those girls were her sisters, united in brutality and detachment. A fierce love developed between them. Practical girls, by necessity. No silliness, no games. Each specially selected at the trains by the commandant himself: only the most exotic and slender, with the blackest hair, the creamiest Jew skin, the darkest almondine Jew eyes, the highest Jew cheekbones.

Say this for the commandant: he had excellent taste. Some of the officers were genuinely fond of the girls, brought them gifts. Jam, a ribbon, music box, perfume. Part of the trick was to act so each man believed he was your one and only.

And when it's all over the Red Cross comes in and hands out oatmeal. She meets my grandfather in a refugee camp. He is a kind and gentle man, a superlative man, not interested in fucking, much too destroyed by his own survival, of which no one knows—or has ever told—the details.

He was ancient by the time I knew him. He'd been married with a daughter already when the war happened. The war. Always a war, always some war. The wife and daughter obviously didn't make it out.

He's my password for everything: *IsaacRadnor36*. Lucky number. Chai times two. How old he was when the war was over.

He'd pat my head absently, slip me a quarter, load up his plate, shuffle to and from the buffet. He didn't say much. I remember him laughing with me once about something silly, the two of us in brief lockstep. He felt like a very silly very elderly brother more than anything else. Funny little old man. *It's your ever-loving grandpa,* he'd say in his thick accent. *It's your ever-loving granddaughter,* I'd faithfully reply.

I do not like talking to the grown-ups, he told me once. *The grown-ups are boring. You are not boring, bubbeleh.* Longest I ever heard him speak. He was dead before I was ten.

I liked how I got special treatment on Holocaust Remembrance Day at school. Me and Tricia Ginsburg and Daniel What-was-his-name, too. I liked how the facts of my family made me unimpeachable in small ways, socially. You just said Holocaust, you just said Survivor, and it was like *I have my period.* You got the equivalent of *poor thing, go lie down in the nurse's office, take it easy.*

But war has destroyed a lot of people in history, I challenged my mother one day after a sixth-grade history unit on Vietnam. It wasn't just the Jews. What about Hiroshima? What about every back-to-back war since forever? What about Palestine? This was meant to bait her.

You don't know the horrors, my mother said, lashing out, meaner the sicker she got, or maybe sicker the meaner she got. *You cannot begin to imagine the horrors. You have no idea. Absolutely none. So just keep your fucking mouth shut, why don't you.*

Anyway, Grandfather adores Grandmother no end, wants to take care of her, is extremely tender. They marry but barely touch for months. They head for Lady Liberty with her outstretched et cetera. Stand-up guy, my grandfather. Smart. Steady. Miraculously cheerful, despite it all. One of those *I believe people are really good at heart* types. And with quite a knack for real estate, turns out. He starts with a single tenement as soon as he can scrape together a down payment from managing a print shop, and within ten years he owns the printing business and two warehouse buildings in SoHo.

Then their problems begin.

I met my best best friend Molly at a party when we were both twenty-three. We had friends in common, don't remember exactly. College grads in the big shitty. Adorable stupid depressed hilarious Molly.

Your basic shtetl sweetheart. Sturdy and symmetrical. Athletic. Cool, gray eyes. Prettiest girl at Jewish day school, hands down. Which is kind of like saying tallest guy at midget conference, but hey. Legs like tree trunks, which a lot of men, it turned out, against the dictates of the women's magazines, did not mind At All. I'm talking no taper from thigh to foot, and she was kind of touchy about it.

She dressed like crap, had no interest in what to wear or how to wear it, no style to speak of, maintained this irritating coterie of vapid Jewish youth-group girlfriends she mocked constantly. Posed no threat to the Jewish youth cohort because of the absent style and tree-trunk legs and elaborate self-mocking, thus was universally adored.

Jesus, she was adorable.

Half-insane, undeniable sparkle in her eye. She was depressed, to be sure, but somehow still bubbly. How the hell do you manage to be both depressed *and* bubbly? Charm, it's called. When she laughed the breath of life breezed through. And if you could make her giggle—which, I was ecstatic to discover, I could! Easily!—it was like a spring you stumble upon, parched.

Don't remember what we talked about that night, only that we stuck together for hours, nursing weak drinks, agreeing that the party was lame, watching the others get progressively more fucked up. We laughed, I remember laughing. We focused single-mindedly on each other's amusement. Which is a way of falling in love. Molly and I had the same sense of humor. This is comparatively rare, I understood with her, because it had never happened to me before. Crazy dorky depressed perverse goofball sluts, us two, vested with a taste for the absurd. I adored her. She was *smart.* Not smart as in has all the answers, smart as in funny and a downer and childlike and honest and enthusiastic. Smart as in asked the necessary questions. Couldn't *lie* about herself, was not putting on a *show.* You looked in those pretty gray eyes, and there she was: *bam,* right there. No scrim, no filter, no bullshit. She wasn't all bound up in there, gagged and furious and resentful beneath some high-pitched shrink-wrapped mess of pleasantry. Unlike the youth-group coterie. All her struggle and sorrow and absurdity, right up front. She wasn't employing some manufactured version of herself as full-time press agent for the *real* self, the agoraphobic coward loner living in a deep psychic cave, see? This was a girl who could not lie about herself. I loved her immediately.

We were both living in terrible apartments, working our first "real" jobs. She had a two-hundred-square-foot basement studio in the East Village; I had a random roommate from Jew camp in Cobble Hill. Corpulent girl a year ahead of me who blew-dry her gel-stiff curls every morning at seven with a diffuser attachment the size of her head, then marched off to her administrative assistant job at NYU Hillel. She was not a bad girl, my roommate, just uninteresting. Almost interestingly uninteresting. Her big rebellion was in refusing to have her hair chemically straightened. She wore a shitload of perfume, whatever designer paperweight they were shilling at the department store that year. Her dad was paying her rent. As was mine, but it was different, because I did not diffuse my hair or wear perfume! Because I was not on the husband hunt! Because I was fucking anonymous men in bar bathrooms and doing any drug offered me and generally Living Life to the Fullest!! The excess of perfume made my skull throb. I wasn't very nice to her.

Molly was fetching coffee on the set of a terrible TV show, but she dreamt of doing stand-up, becoming Tina Fey.

Her parents were career Jews, big *machers* in the suburban DC Jewish community, confounded by her sensibility.

My "alternative lifestyle," she said, rolling those pretty gray eyes. Meaning disinclination to go to social work school and/or find a husband—any husband! Strike that: any rich Jewish husband!—ASAP.

Also there was the issue of her intermittent breakdowns, her abiding fondness for her shrink, her string of barely paying jobs. She confounded those *machers*. In theory they were supportive of her stand-up dreams, but she never let them come see her perform in the tiny comedy clubs where she got the worst time slots.

I was fetching coffee for a film producer, meanwhile. He'd had some success in the eighties with a blockbuster romantic comedy about a goofy guy who builds himself a clumsy, malfunctioning robot girlfriend. There were three (and counting) sequels. Straight-to-video stuff, but vast foreign markets were dying for more.

Maybe I'll sleep with your boss so he'll produce my one-woman show.

Is that how it works?

That, my friend, is precisely how it works.

My favorite bit she did was this one where the refrain was *omigod thanks daddy am I right?* First a description of some scrape she'd gotten into, your basic wacky sluttery in the big shitty—genital warts from a one-night stand with an investment banker, kicked out of her apartment for hosting a party during which someone OD'd in the hallway, fired from her job for talking shit about her boss in monitored email—and describe the way her semi-clueless dad had gotten her out of it while keeping it secret from her mom. The subtext was amazing—she was a hopeless daddy's girl, and there was no way any other man could ever begin to compete. Hence the lovelorn angle. She had endless ways of changing up the lilt and intonation of it.

Omigod. Thanks daddy. Am I right? Ohhhhhhhhhmigod. Thanksdaddyami right? Omigodthanksdaddyamiright?

You're so good, I'd say. She didn't believe me.

People dismissed her as a Sarah Silverman rip-off, but she was funny in her own right. More descendant than rip-off, to be sure.

Silverman's a talentless cunt, she'd say. *Fucked her way up.* Which was a sort of funny critique, as Molly was concurrently inviting the terrible talk-show host over Sunday nights to spank her and do some blow.

It's not as if there's only room for one adorable fucked-up Jewish girl comedian in the world, I reminded her.

She'd get up there looking so pretty, so wholesome, so sweet and doe-eyed, you wanted to hold her hand and run through a field of wildflowers. There would be genuine fear in her eyes, she made no effort to disguise it, so you just loved her all the more. Proverbial deer in headlights. Then she'd say, *I'm so much happier with my appearance since I had my beard removed.*

Or *Even if my ex-boyfriend* hadn't *raped me, I'd probably say he did 'cause then you'd feel all bad for me. And when people feel bad for you, they're really sweet and then they seriously leave you so very alone, no one bugs you at all. If you want some privacy, just get super depressed and wounded, it's amazing, people just immediately drop you altogether and you can get some phenomenal peace and quiet . . . in which to contemplate how best to off yourself.*

We were miserable, but miserable together. There were drinks and dinners, there were gatherings on weekends. There were friends of friends throwing parties, connections at fun restaurants and bars. There were shows and excursions. Brunch and brunch and brunch. There were lovers and love interests and a guy from the other night, no, no, the *other* other night, in endless supply.

But the years were not kind.

Her old cohort began to send out save-the-dates, plotted elaborate showers. Our twenties were on the wane, and it was assumed that after the stand-up silliness she'd find a nice (rich, Jewish) husband online and come back home to plan a wedding with her mom and have some babies. She owned her twenties, went the unspoken deal; they owned her after that. She loathed her mother and on occasion had no trouble telling her mother where to shove those vapid projections, but Daddy she couldn't disappoint. She couldn't break Daddy's heart. She hated herself for being conventional, but the life-on-her-terms clock was running out. Tapped for bridesmaid duty by one after another of the cohort.

I applied to grad school and got in. Impressed with myself for kicking theoretical feminist ass, and on a fellowship to boot. I started hanging out with Marianne.

Molly began to watch the comics with whom she'd started out get somewhere, one an assistant in the writers' room at *Saturday Night Live,* another opening on a huge college tour, a third recently cast in the ensemble of a new TV show.

I took up with Paul; Molly switched to a new antidepressant cocktail on which she was forbidden to drink. She drank anyway. She'd fuck someone and be depressed for days when he didn't call. She'd pore over the Sunday *Times* wedding announcements and threaten suicide whenever one of her former classmates turned up. She couldn't manage to finish the spec script she needed to land a proper entry-level writing gig, and so she floundered in the shitty gopher pool as a fresh new wave of people showed up from the Ivy League. She drank and drank. She was broke. Her parents wanted her to go to grad school. It didn't matter what kind. They wanted her to pick a kind of grad school and go to it. There she'd meet her husband. And turn into her mother, who did not stop talking for literally five minutes the first time I met her. Daddy was quiet, charged with power and authority. Kind of hot.

She called weeping over the wedding announcements one June Sunday.

It's never going to happen for me.

What is never going to happen for you, honey?

Paul was naked in my sheets, casually holding my right foot in his armpit while he read the automotive section. Never before or since have I seen anyone read the automotive section.

Molly whimpered.

Look, I said. Way past bored. *It's your life, babe. Do what you want or do what they want, but don't torture yourself.* I had been repeating some version of this for months. The depressed are such a bore!

I pulled away, I guess. Guilty. I ignored her calls. She'd whine about her parents and the latest insulting bridal shower and the inferior comic who sold a script and the other inferior comic who had a show in development and the current destination-wedding invitation and the guy who didn't call when he said he'd call.

When she wasn't blackout drinking and sucking dick for a better time slot, she biked (sans helmet) all over the city. Her long hair would fly behind her, and you'd think: that girl is amazing. If only that girl had the first clue how amazing she is.

Everything in your *life seems to be working out just swell,* she said. Like I was the enemy. Like I hadn't suffered. Slowly then suddenly I saw that she had only liked me because I was as miserable as she was.

She finally did move to LA and we didn't speak for a year and then she moved back from LA and didn't call me and then I saw her somewhere and she ignored me and so I ignored her.

Then there was nothing between us anymore.

No us.

Paul kept the mood light waiting around for labor to begin, waiting and waiting and waiting, with our giant old thesaurus. I was not simply huge. I was arched, bellied, biconvex, bloated, bold, bombous, bossed, bosselated, bossy, bowed, bulbiform, bulbous, clavated, corniform, cornute, gibbous, hemispheric, hummocky, in relief, lenticular, lentiform, maniform, nodular, odontoid, papulous, projecting, prominent, protuberant, raised, salient, tuberculous, tuberous, timorous.

He got out his guitar and made up a song. I took issue with *bossy,* and somewhere between *bulbiform* and *odontoid* the whole thing began to sound kind of obnoxious. You get sort of oversensitive toward the end.

My due date passed, and officially we were behind schedule. They ordered a sonogram, looked for problems, told us about possibilities of problems. Made concerned faces and laid out the unacceptable possibilities.

Standard practice.

You hear enough *monitor, low-fluid, toxicity, big, proactive, posterior, count kicks, strip membranes,* and you think, Jesus, okay, fuck, do whatever you have to do, whatever you people *say,* just make it okay.

Even though I had told that goddamn OB I wanted to "try" for a normal birth.

Sure, he'd said. Nothing bad was going to happen to me with *this* guy on duty. *Give it a try. I'm all for that. That's great. So you're a tough girl. Gonna muscle through.*

I played along, practically batted my lashes.

I'd like to try.

Good for you. He turned to Paul. *I like that. Tough cookie.*

And fine: I had failed to watch the documentaries. I was superstitious. I didn't want to jinx things. I was overwhelmed. I never got around to it.

(*Lazy,* my mother says. *Always were.*)

Folks. Here's the husky OB, dude I had once, just one time, early on, imagined bending me over his desk and fucking me graduate school style. (Ode to the pregnant libido.)

It is upon us to get this show on the road. Sexy salt-and-pepper, scrubs, fluorescent rubber gardening clogs. Congenial enough, confidence like a birthright. *Baby's gettin' pretty big. Looks pretty well cooked. Don't want him getting much bigger. Lots can start to go wrong. We need to take this show on the road. You ready to meet your baby?*

I mean, listen. Historically I got that you had to own your

body, that they'd take it from you and tell you not to trouble your pretty little head about it. I'm supposedly on my way to a doctorate in women's studies, for shit's sake. I had some awareness that Barbara Ehrenreich had done early work on midwifery, the witch hunts, the medical industry's treatment of women's issues. I'd heard Ani DiFranco had given birth at home.

But there I was: huge, disoriented, impatient, scared. Bellied, biconvex, bloated. I handed myself over. Gave them my precious protuberance to deal with as they saw fit.

Yes, I'm ready to have this baby.

No more free lunches for the little one, joked an obese nurse in puppy scrubs while hooking me up to the Pitocin drip, which I've since learned is synthesized from cattle pituitary.

Induce: trigger, arouse, wheedle into, set in motion, cajole, encourage, prompt, prod, prevail, spur, generate, instigate, trigger, engender, foster, occasion.

Move by force.

I mean, we use *motherfucker* in all sorts of contexts. We're pretty liberal nowadays in our collective use of the word *motherfucker*. But let's corral it now, shall we? Reclaim it. If you are an obstetrician or obstetrical nurse and your C-section rate is over, say, 9 percent, you are henceforth an official motherfucker.

I pity you, Mina says, her eyes wet and sincere.

Well, that's direct. It stings. Pity is so goddamn inescapable, infinitely sadder than scorn.

It's clear that winter isn't going anywhere. We can't simply wait it out inside. We're getting antsy and there's supposedly some major storm coming tomorrow.

There's this place.

I like places.

Road trip. The old mill in a tiny town called Victory. Used to be a textile mill. Opened in 1846. Closed in 1989, and sayonara, town. Goodbye, people. Hello, rot.

The co-op kids are talking about planning yet another benefit this summer to help pay for its conversion to an arts center. Which is so incredibly adorable of them, because from the looks of it Donald Trump would have to take out about seventeen mortgages to salvage this ruin.

They want to call it "the Downriver."

Why?

Factories were usually built downriver with the town upriver. So the pollution from the factory wouldn't poison everyone.

Well, eventually poison everyone.

Not for a couple generations, though.

So, no biggie.

This is not a cool town. No espresso, no hand-spun textiles, no vintage shops. This is not one of those secret hipster hideouts. Sweet enclaves where you can find well-dressed arty fuckers with kids named Zenith, Phoenix, Fidel; this is not one of those. This is a murdered corpse of a town. This is a decline-of-the-empire town.

The mill is expansive, room after abandoned room, sprawling. I used to go to the mall to get good and numb. Buy some underwear, eat something synthetic, drive home stupefied as an overfed farm animal on an indefinite course of antibiotics, forcibly separated from my young.

This is way better.

We wear the babies. Zev is asleep on her front and Walker's asleep on my back. Postindustrial mountaineers, bundled against the cold. We're on the third floor, probably forty feet from the ground. Ahead, the entire south wall of the place is gone and wood plank floor slopes off into thin air. I want to get closer, to peek over the edge, taste the fear, but Mina has my arm tight.

You're supposed to take your baby to windowless baby gyms or basement baby music class or whatever the fuck. Not out into the actual grim, broken world, where glass might cut and the floor might collapse and there's money to be made in fresh ugliness every day.

The whole world is new, she says. *It's an entirely new place. It's the craziest. I don't think I'll ever be bored again.*

A dried-out yellow wall calendar from 1989. Time officially stopped.

It's balls cold.

We head back down the stairwell into a huge open space with floor-to-ceiling windows. Metal columns. Five hundred people probably worked in this room. She points out sheets of ice on the floor below a stretch of missing windows.

Women without sisters are at a marked disadvantage, I say.

And women with crappy sisters! she says.

It seems like the band might have been a kind of sisterhood.

She shrugs. *For a little while. Early on. Then it wasn't. Anyway, we really weren't that good.*

We make our way out, stepping over slippery frozen patches, scattered glass.

What are you talking about? Everyone loved you.

Maybe. But we weren't that good.

She stops to catch her breath.

We were like . . . short stories about writers of short stories.

Those can be good.

I mean, it was this inside joke. We only had something to offer people playing at being people. There was nothing at stake. Irony isn't some new thing, you know? We weren't being sincere. And when you're young, insincerity seems like this grand discovery? This noble fuck-you?

But it's just a way of wasting time.

Kelly was pure, so it destroyed her straight off. But Stef bought into the hype. The littlest bit of recognition, no matter how small, just fired her so up. That was all she wanted. Her picture taken, her name in the paper.

Yeah, I say. *Well. Karma's a bitch.*

I kind of envied her. Wouldn't it be fabulous to be so simple?

God, yes.

They sometimes show Kelly's picture alongside Jimi Hendrix and Janis Joplin and Jim Morrison and Kurt Cobain and them all. Dead at twenty-seven. And they always leave out Mia Zapata, biggest badass of all.

Who's Mia Zapata?

Exactly. I bet Stef is irritated to this day that she's not as famous as Kelly.

Or as you.

She laughs.

Don't get me wrong, I was a fucked-up lunatic back then, Mina says. *But that bitch was the Devil.*

Legend has it Mina and Stef had to be physically separated at Kelly's wake. Stef says Mina indirectly killed Kelly by introducing her to heroin, the love of her life; Mina says everyone they knew tried it once. Stef says Kelly never wanted Mina in the band long term; Mina says Stef is a dumb fame whore.

Stef runs her Christian rock camp near Nashville now. *In a way,* she told some local arts rag a while back, *I died and then got clean. I mean not literally died but died in every possible other way except literally.*

A deserted subway platform with Molly, drunk, late night, the Q slow to come. We were on a bench and Molly's half-asleep with her head on my shoulder.

There was a woman loping unsteadily toward us from the other end of the platform. She shambled, she weaved. She stopped halfway to whisper with someone who wasn't there. She was filthy.

I didn't move.

My mother advanced.

What the fuck are you looking at?

I said nothing.

You think I don't have regrets? You think I wanted this??

I couldn't look at her.

I don't know.

You worthless little shit. You think I wanted this? You think I chose this?

I refused to look at her.

Leave me alone.

I won't take your crap, you ungrateful little shit! You think the world owes you something? The world owes you nothing! THE WORLD OWES YOU NOTHING! NOTHING! NOTHING!

My heart slammed: fight or flight? Flight or fight? What kind of pathetically damaged animal decides on . . . neither?

Couldn't breathe. Tried to say *help* but it came out a stupid squeak.

Are you okay? Molly finally wanted to know.

Couldn't answer. Walls closing in.

A person who doesn't have friends must explain himself to strang-

ers, I read in a poem once, and I saw how even my "best" friends were thusly unreal: I had to explain myself constantly, always, to everyone.

Why hadn't she tried harder, my grandmother obsesses. Why hadn't she worked to curry favor with an officer, insinuate herself into his affections, and thereby manage to somehow find and save even *one* of her siblings? Their names she can't even bear to recall. And why can't she stop this obsessing? It's over. It's past. They're in America now. The war is behind them. Another life.

But she's begun to miscarry. Something is very wrong. Her body keeps killing babies. She and my grandfather are getting rich now, really doing their part for the good old Dream. But she keeps leaking would-be fetuses, wakes up screaming, crying, sweating, bleeding.

She is not the *people are really good at heart* type. She wakes from nightmares in which the incinerated siblings shriek for help from a black sinkhole. Nightmares in which an SS officer lines her up with her primary school mates and massacres them all with a hailstorm of bullets coming from his very tiny dick.

Miscarriage after miscarriage, and by the third or fourth it's into the loony bin for her. Back then a strong breeze could get a girl committed.

A rest, the doctor assures my confounded grandfather. *A short rest will do her wonders.*

Every family had one, batshit great-aunt, whatever. Even the Kennedys! Tie her down, force the tranquilizers, restart her brain. Take out her damned brain if all else fails.

Schizoid truth tellers, tortured soothsayers, haunted intuitives, furious denied lesbians.

She got two rounds of electroshock.

A mild case, the doctor says, satisfied. No lobotomy. She is sent home to the new house in Westchester so she can continue the "rest" in the "country."

Maybe now they will have their baby.

Enter the miracle doctor.

Enter the miracle drug.

And less than a year later, the terrifying tiny baby girl. A daughter.

But first: childbirth, midcentury American style. On sale half an hour downriver, at the good antique shops.

Now the nurses have her strapped down, drugged and thrashing, crying out, welts where the restraints hold her wrists and ankles. The masked nurses appear, disappear, reappear. One pushes down hard on her belly. The doctor arrives, selects his cutting instrument, and separates her with one neat movement. She can feel it, even though she's not supposed to feel anything. She understands that she has been split at the root, loosened, just not very clearly, not clearly enough to know it's *her,* precisely.

No good, being strapped down, heart racing, looking for the nurse, please, someone. She sobs, desperate. Tries to speak. No one hears her. The thing insists from within that *it* knows best. What kind of thing would do this to her? After their quite lovely time living together these ten months? She can feel it, so insistent.

She is thirsty. She will surely die of thirst. What wouldn't she give for a drink. *Water,* she tries to say, *water.* They ignore her. Are they angry with her? Has she done something wrong? She has done so much wrong. She tries to say *water,* but no one understands. The thing wants out. The thing is trying to get out. It's monstrous. *Please,* she tries. *Oh please help me.*

Now the doctor wields another shiny instrument, big impressive one, opens and closes. A kind of trap. Two masked nurses hold her down. They terrify her. She can't see their faces. A third pushes on her belly as the doctor goes in with those steel jaws, and this is his favorite part, oh yes, in past his nice, clean incision, clamp that soft head and give it a good tug.

The insistent incredible terrifying monstrous thing is removed from her.

Perfect! says the doctor, holding it by its ankles. He smacks it so it shrieks and gasps and shakes, all purple. The doctor loves his job. Little lungs hard at work right away, yes, good, just what he likes to see. Ten fingers, ten toes.

They hold it up for her to see and then they spirit the thing away. An echo of its yelping remains. She has heard that sound before because she has *made* that sound, a long time ago, or not so long ago.

The new mother is half-conscious, vomiting, shaking, eyes searching frantically, blindly, for what? The doctor stitches her up and is gone.

Véronique and Helge never made it out, by the way. Mere weeks before liberation they went on a walk together on the outskirts of camp, just a quick taste of air, sharing a precious cigarette: so stupid, so arrogant! An idiotic Kapo didn't recognize the officers' vaunted whores, just saw two Jew girls and shot them both dead on the spot.

Later, for good measure, the commandant and a few senior officers beat the living shit out of that Kapo. The memory of Véronique's perfect pink pussy spurred them into a frenzy.

But my mother's mother survived, yes she sure did. Made it to America, to electroshock, to DES, to scopolamine. Tied to a bed in a different country, begging for someone to help her in a language no one could understand.

Husband, where is her husband, he's not here, he's not allowed. They're giving her another injection now. Another drug, lead fist. Muted pain, it turns out, is much worse than clear pain. Clear pain is quantifiable. One can face it, reckon with it, come away braver. There is no way to understand what you cannot feel. No reckoning to be had. It will haunt you forever, make you afraid. Still, they call her this laughable word: *Survivor.*

Eighteen years later she sticks her head in the oven. Amazing she made it that long.

The perfect baby girl, my mother, got a call on the Wellesley dorm hall phone.

A Survivor no more.

The girls in grad school hated me. They all wanted to be Marianne's favorite, but only I was Marianne's favorite.

At first I wanted to use feminist theory as a lens through which to read literature.

Marianne dismissed novels: *irrelevant, because they are forever going on and on about the things around* the *thing; if they actually attempted to* name *the thing, all that narrative would become immediately inconsequential. Novelists know this. It's the bread and butter of storytelling. Stories are where people go when they don't have the tenaciousness to go straight to the heart of the matter in a scientific manner. Stories are a rehearsal, an avoidance of politics and activism and rage and grief. A way for the writer to remove herself from the real problem.*

So . . . you think I shouldn't go for an MFA?

We'd have dinner, lots of wine. She had me to her house upstate. More wine. Her glamorous life, her many lovers. The most important of whom, a painter, had recently died. They hadn't lived together; he'd had a wife, a grown family, the works. But they'd been involved on and off for years. She was vague about the details. I had a hunch he bought her the upstate house. So what.

She wasn't the baby-having type. She was uninterested in baby having. She'd lost too many friends to baby having.

They were good women, she'd say. More matter-of-fact than bitter.

Her work was about how we look at women, how we understand and own them by looking at them. The various ways a necessarily self-conscious woman appropriates this, to her benefit or detriment.

Yes, I thought when I read her in preparation for her seminar. Yesssssss. She'd made her name with that stuff in the eighties, though now it's taken so for granted, she doesn't really get her due. In her office I noticed a Barbara Kruger postcard tacked up over her desk. *Your gaze hits the side of my face.* She took it down and gave it to me. It's on my fridge even now, yellowing.

She was riveting. Places she'd been, people she knew. I sat myself directly at her feet. What should I think? How should I feel?

When I finished my master's, she gave me her grandfather's pocket watch. When I published that first big-deal article, a garnet brooch of her grandmother's. *I never had a daughter,* she wrote in a small note made from a three-inch-high thrift store black-and-white photograph of a blurry, bonneted baby.

No choice but to take it as a compliment when the other girls hate you: you must be hot shit. Still, they hated me. Also because their boyfriends wanted to fuck me.

One of the girls especially did not like me. She had it out for me. I found this hilarious. I was no threat! Not *really.* Not *actually.* What kind of moron did she have to be to imagine me a threat? At base I hate myself so much I can barely speak! Hate myself so much that to this very day I sometimes can't manage to get dressed. So the fuck what if I fucked your stupid fucking boyfriend? Be mad at your mediocre boyfriend, sweetie-pants. But you had to kind of love that girl. You can always at least sort of love whatever you fully understand.

Then there was Anna, always a weird one. Just starting the program as I was on my way out. WASP. Cut off from something essential, earthy. Doing some best imitation of life. Anorectic's anorectic. True hunger artist, to the bone. Never dated until a few years later, in her late twenties, when she was adjuncting in a midsized city in the South and took up with the vice president of a local bank. A man whose quirk was to insist she grow her nails extremely long and make sure they were perfectly manicured at all times. He was willing to pay for weekly manicures, he told her on their first or second date. She was fine with it, though more than a little sheepish.

I know how it sounds, she told me. *He's an interesting guy. But I know how it sounds.*

Whatever, I said.

I know. I know. But he's nice. I like him.

Last I saw her I was pregnant. We had dinner. (*I* had dinner.) She confessed a deep, abiding fear of pregnant bellies.

They disgust me, actually, she said.

After the birth I never heard from her. Nothing. I called her in a sorry state with the stroller alone on a bench in the park one day, wanting to tell her everything, if only she'd pick up. She was smart, and smart ones aren't easy to come by. She never called back.

I sat on that cold park bench for a while, couldn't think of anyone else to call. Do you slowly lose everyone? Do you just get lonelier and lonelier until you die?

I tried again a few months later. She answered that time—*Heyyyyy! How are you?*—polite, distant.

I actually can't talk right now, she said, *but can I call you in, like, ten minutes?* Specious bitch!

Sure thing, I said.

Still waiting for that call.

Anyway, no matter. It's not personal. You don't go to funerals because you can't deal with going to funerals. Because you're scared, inept, phobic. Shrink-wrapped in your own smallness. Because you can't handle it. You might even be ashamed of yourself for failing to show up at the funeral. But sorry, you're just not the kind of person who goes to funerals. Also known as an asshole.

When I broke the news to Marianne that I was pregnant, she gazed out her office window, took a drag off a cigarette, angled a long, graceful exhale.

Well. If that's. What you think. You want.

• • •

Looking at some Firestone on the stoop for twenty minutes before it's time to get Walker. Some second-wave bullshit about how biology isn't destiny. Defeat the female body and be liberated from it.

I'd like to send around a paper on this with a long, involved academic title. The entirety of the piece would just read: Bullshit! Bullshit! Bullshit! Bullshit! Bullshit!

It's a clear day, and I'm sitting with my face to the sun. I can see my breath. But the sun, the sun, the sun!

Cat comes up the block pushing a stroller. Apparently the woman next door to her has a new baby.

She just needed a couple hours to herself, Cat tells me authoritatively.

And you're helping her out.

Her smile is beatific.

You've found yourself another friend, it conveys, and so, so, so have I, I, I.

Are you fucking joking? Are you kidding me right now?

What?

Nothing. That's really nice of you. Good.

A house fell down on Main Street. A nineteenth-century brick row house. Most of the façade and the southeastern wall of the thing. Looks like a dollhouse now. All the rooms are visible from the front. There was work being done on the house next door, and you know how sometimes when they mess with the foundation of a two-hundred-year-old house the one next door decides to fall down? It's like the house says oh great here we go again with another round of these jerks, another generation of assholes making noise; I think I'll call it a day.

I stand across the street for a while with like thirty other people watching the trucks and the flashing lights. Walker asleep in the stroller.

I loved that dollhouse my father got me the first time my mother was sick. Getting to see inside the whole house, inside every room, all those private spaces that make up the life of a family. I was godlike, omniscient. I knew every corner of that house. All its goings-on were so, so small and so very manageable as compared with mine. No unknown rooms, no known but uninhabitable ones.

Agonizingly new baby at the co-op.

How old's your baby?

Just about two weeks.

Tiniest person. The mom is not friendly. Does it cost her *money* to smile?

The baby's big brother runs up and kisses her face, runs off again.

Her protector, the dad says. I nod.

Lucky girl.

Naomi hands me a flyer when my shift's over.

Gonna be amazeballs this month. Bunch of farmers from Germantown are joining up, gonna start a monthly CSA tie-in. How great is that? You can pick up your produce at the party!

In January the CSA consists exclusively of potatoes and onions and kohlrabi, but I do like it up here, in theory.

My lame book, Mina says when I finally tell her how much I adore it.

It's not lame. I really loved it.

Thank you. That's nice to hear.

I mean, and it was kind of a big deal, wasn't it?

To you, I guess.

We both know quite well her book's a big deal. I'm pretending otherwise so she won't think I'm a culture vulture. Only decent to make believe you don't know how to use the Internet. Pretend you can't find out all sorts of shit about people before you actually get to know them. Or in lieu of actually getting to know them.

She shrugs. She won't trade on it. Not a trace of arrogance.

Maybe I'd feel better about it if it'd been less of a big deal. It just fucks with you, how people fall all over themselves being nice to you all of a sudden. They write you off as a crazy bitch for years, then suddenly they stop and pay attention and reward you for being a crazy bitch. Complete mindfuck. And speaking of mindfuck. Turns out we're going to Brooklyn at the end of the month.

Like, to visit?

No.

I would rather she just hit me in the face.

Wait, you're going to Brooklyn to live?

For now.

But. What? Why? Crisp and Jerry aren't coming home for another six months.

The gig is over. And this town is kind of a shithole, and my sister's being weirdly nice.

They already have sisters, the best girls. If you can find a girl to love, it'll turn out she already has a sister.

So you're going to Brooklyn. To live.

My sister has a lot of space.

Ooh, like a brownstone?

She has a lot of space.

But you have a community here.

By which I mean, *I* have a community here, and it's *you.*

This was always temporary.

I just thought.

Brooklyn's not that far.

Seriously, though? Brooklyn?

What's wrong with Brooklyn? But she can't even keep a straight face long enough to get past the "Brook."

Wow, dude.

My sister's been really amazing the last few weeks on the phone. Really supportive.

You'll just love living among the bourgeoisie. Such good people. Salt of the earth.

She's my sister.

I'm your sister, you fucking whore.

Don't be weird.

Do you not understand what my life was like before you?

I do, she says.

You are going to completely despise it there.

You're probably right.

Whatever, no, go live a highly curated little life along with all the other highly curated little lifers.

My sister wants to help. I think she misses when her kids were little. And this way the kids get to know each other. And she lives in a giant house, and her marriage sounds like it's just about over . . .

So what'd you put a fucking spell on me for?

You saved my life.

How nice for you.

Another one bites the dust. This house can't be salvaged. Gonna have to tear it all down.

• • •

At pickup I am fleetingly overcome with wanting Nasreen's stepson. Built, broad, twenty-five, tattoo sleeves in brilliant colors on both arms, radiates sex.

It takes me by surprise, the wanting, and I understand that in some way I am better.

I don't need her.

Forget her.

You okay? Paul wants to know in the thirty seconds before he's asleep.

Don't be one of those women who bitch to their husbands about other women all the time, my mother advises in singsong. *Men do not care about the dramas of women and are exhausted by women who do.* She's trying to be helpful. And she's actually not wrong.

I'm fine. I say.

What? What's the matter?

My good Paul.

Spare him, my mother croons.

But you can't complain to the source of your complaint, so.

She's leaving.

Who's leaving?

He's snoring before I can answer.

A night in the city again.

On the train down I'm sitting next to some fifteen-year-old texting texting texting the whole way. Hate these little girls because they never have to be alone with themselves. Life is going to be so fucking cruel to you, you prissy little bitch.

So it seems I'm the kind of old person who hates young people. This is a bad sign.

I'm crashing at Erica and Steve's, because it's free and luxe and huge and there are views and I figure I owe them a visit. It's decorated like an expensive, of-the-moment hotel.

Hey wow your tits look semi-normal again. I got used to seeing them so freakishly huge, Erica says before hello. She is wearing the scariest shoes I have ever seen. *What? What? I'm saying your tits look good! Don't be so fucking touchy.*

I'm fond of Steve, it turns out. He's a shameless good time. Ribald, hilarious goofball undercover stoner with the most abhorrent politics you can possibly imagine. I can't help it; I'm fond of the dude.

He's gotten into fancy-cocktail making, simian brow all knotted in deep focus for the twenty minutes it takes him to mix us some drinks.

But the other thing about Steve is the sense that because I am a female he can't immediately classify, I set him more or less on edge. Call it low-grade misogyny. It's not extreme-porno misogyny, not I'm-gonna-rape-and-kill-you misogyny, just plain old run-of-the-mill semiconscious women-are-to-fuck-or-mother misogyny. Fear of the female. Menstrual cycle as mysterious sinister secret, et cetera. Women as doormats and/or commodities and/or hookers, the end. Intuition an absurdity. Life only and always about what we can touch/articulate/own. And me with my insistence on eye contact, my opinions! My candor! My always! Feeling! So! Much! Something about how these kinds of men would never dream of hanging out with a woman for fun, talking to a woman just because her perspective on life is inherently valuable. Not, at least, if he wasn't also hoping to fuck her.

There's this college-dropout friend of Paul's. Professional jazz musician. We saw him play a few years ago. So talented. His wife had left him for another guy, and you got the sense he sort of blamed you for it, because you too were female. Or maybe it was that personhood was not a privilege granted a female automatically. You had to earn it, overcome the fact of your lips, your breasts, your cunt, your ass. Say something witty and smart, include some esoteric reference, prove you were not, at heart, a simple harlot, and thusly earn personhood. Women are foreign, unpredictable. Do not talk to a woman. Do not get caught in her web. Fundamentally she makes no sense. She will pull you under, fry up your cock in a pan and eat it for breakfast along with some eggs.

But Steve's all right, especially stoned. *Really* loves his surround sound. He hands me my elaborate cocktail.

You guys aren't drinking?

Erica grins. Steve grins.

Oh my God.

Yuuuuup!

Oh, I say, tearing up. *Sweetheart.*

I hold my glass out for a toast.

May you learn to mother yourself as you learn to mother your child, I say. *May you trust and respect your body, and may others trust and respect your body, and may your body astound you.*

What she said, Steve says, pretending to knock one back. *That was hella deep, Ari, wow.*

Later I meet Subeena for a drink. She talks at me for an hour about why now would be a good time for her to freeze her eggs because she's getting promoted at the blog. She does not ask me a single question.

Return to Steve and Erica's at midnight. All the lights are on.

You guys?

They're asleep, sprawled across their gigantic bed. Erica's wearing a silk eye mask, and their pug is gnawing ecstatically on a bone at the foot of the bed. The huge television is blaring a reality show about crazy sad enraged bejeweled old women with too much money.

Train home, I get a good seat on the river side. Sun is setting. Everyone sucks. The lady in the row ahead, sick and coughing and obviously contagious. The guy who takes my ticket, so swaggery and obviously a rapist.

Nina Simone is singing, *No use old girl / You might as well surrender.*

It wasn't just Cat and the dead-eyed faculty wife. There was the competitive yoga instructor two towns over. There was the moms' group and the whole *other* moms' group. I'm telling you, I tried. I'd be friends with Hitler if he wanted to have a chill playdate. You have to find people, people with babies, and you might not technically like these people, but you'll be so grateful for the shorthand, any blessed shorthand, that it won't seem to matter. But it *will* matter, because you'll be lonely, and come to feel terrifically fragmented, and death might come to seem like a relief.

A baby opens you up, is the problem. No way around it unless you want to pay someone else to have it for you. There's before and there's after. To live in your body before is one thing. To live in your body after is another. Some deal by attempting to micromanage; some go crazy; some zone right the hell on out. Or all of the above. A blessed few resist any of these, and when you meet her, you'll know her immediately by the look in her eyes: weary, humbled, wobbly but still standing. Present, if faintly. You don't meet her often.

Postcard from Crispin.

hiya how r u booberoo, i miss our consciousness-raisings. R u being good 2 yrslf? we r in montepulciano and it is fucked up beautiful. Love you. XOXO

They've been together twenty years, Crisp and Jer. Crisp's first partner died in the eighties, of the plague. Gorgeous photo of him in the living room. Jer doesn't mind in the least. He saw me staring at the photo once.

What a beauty, huh?

Why didn't Crisp get the plague, too? Freak luck. They have no idea. Rare mystery. He tries not to think about it.

It's the covered-dish brigade! I'd hear Jerry calling from our stoop, arms too full of food and wine to ring the bell.

They saved me.

You saved yourself, gorgeous, Crisp said. *You just needed a little help laughing about it.*

Two hundred years ago—hell, one hundred years ago—you'd have a child surrounded by other women: your mother, her mother, sisters, cousins, sisters-in-law, mother-in-law. And you'd be a teenager, too young to have had any kind of life yourself. You'd share childcare with a raft of women. They'd help you, keep you company, show you how. Then you'd do the same. Not just people to share in the work of raising children, but people to share in the loving of children.

Now maybe you make a living, maybe you get to know yourself on your own terms. Maybe you have adventures, heartbreak. Maybe you nurture ambition. Maybe you explore your sexuality. And then: unceremoniously sliced in fucking half, handed a newborn, home to your little isolation tank, get on with it, and don't you dare post too many pictures. You don't want to be one of *those*.

Paul meant well. Paul is the embodiment of decency. But Paul couldn't help me. You have to know what people are capable of, and forgive them for whatever they're not.

It'll keep getting easier, Jer assured me.

How do you know? I asked him.

I had six older sisters, hon. I'm a Catholic faggot from Georgia. I stuttered so bad, I barely spoke until my late teens. I am intimately familiar with what women go through. My mother had seven children in nine years, one of whom died before his first birthday. I didn't understand that she was catastrophically depressed until she was seventy-five years old traveling around the world on group tours and I saw a photo of her actually smiling for the first time in my life.

Yeah, public service announcement, Crisp said. *If someone you love or just like a lot or just kind of know gives birth to a baby, GO OVER TO HER HOUSE WITH FOOD AND HANG OUT WITH HER on the regular for a while.*

No need to call first, I agreed.

It's like when someone dies, Jer said.

Do not fucking send flowers.

It is exactly like when someone dies. Better get used to it.

We refilled our glasses.

Paul and I got married at Brooklyn Borough Hall and had dinner at our favorite restaurant after.

Molly was there. Erica. My father and Sheryl. Marianne

made an appearance but left after one drink. The old jazz musician friend of Paul's. We invited them a week beforehand: *getting married tuesday! dinner after.* It demanded to be downplayed.

I wore a gold, bias-cut, raw-silk dress made by a woman with a storefront on Atlantic, paired with classic cowboy boots and a vintage black lace bolero jacket. Had my hair up loosely with an enormous red orchid pinned on the left side. I was so proud that night, so self-possessed, standing tall, fully inhabited. I owned myself, felt fully mine to give. I stayed close to Paul, very much his wife. Nothing mattered so much as he and I mattered to each other. Marriage is simply realignment.

Sheryl's wedding gift was a copy of a weird little joke book called *Nice Jewish Goy: Intermarriage and You.* Inscribed to us personally by the author.

Sheryl and Norman were obviously uncomfortable, but they bit their big Jew lips about it. Unlike my crazy aunt Ellen, who sent me that letter about *shame* and *cut off* and *disappointment* and *history* and *your grandparents* and *lost to us.* Real classic of the genre.

She's such a lunatic, Erica said of her mother. *I'm so sorry. She's fucking crazy.*

One of Paul's cousins is married to a Jew. We visited them once, and they had a mezuzah hanging upside down on the wrong side of their front door.

Molly gave a toast. Drunk, needless to say. Something about *how amazing it is when you find the person you're meant to be with, or so I'm told, not that I know anything whatsoever about that, but anyway thanksdaddyamiright?*

My father clinked a knife against a glass when the dinner was over. Dude waited until *dessert* was being cleared.

Ariella. You were the most wonderful surprise of our lives. It was the first time in years he'd come anywhere close to talking about my mother. I waited for more. What else? What about *her?* What *about* her??

Marriage, he went on, *is incredibly easy if you're married to the right person.* He beamed at Sheryl and sat back down, speech over.

Well, that's *obviously total bullshit,* I whispered to Paul. *But I love you.*

Get a room, Molly muttered around midnight. Only she and we were left in the flickering candlelight of that beautiful restaurant, our shoes kicked off, my feet in Paul's lap.

Of course she disliked me when I felt most relaxed and strong. The talk show host had entered rehab and disappeared. My happiness was a betrayal.

She left to go to a party in Brooklyn Heights.

Realignment.

I gather my best materials on the subject, even the documentary I myself failed to watch, and put the package in the mail to Erica. Man is she lucky to have me. Wish *I'd* had me.

Now I zap her a link: "Top Ten Signs Your Doctor Is Planning an Unnecessary C-Section."

invaluable resource! hope you're feeling good! lots of love! p.s. watch the documentary!

Two seconds later her reply.

know it comes from place of love but I'm stressed enuff and you need to cease and desist, thanks! ;)

Fucking *winky* face!?

Give me a break. I tap furiously:

Please educate yourself. Knowledge is good, promise.

I have a plan that works for me n steve & need you to respect that!

Oh, right, sure, cool, okay. A plan wherein you pretend it's 1950 and get knocked the fuck out and come to with offspring and set about pretending the whole ordeal never happened. A *plan.*

I'm actually shaking with rage. Vapid twat! Shaking, I am! Amazing, what the body can do.

What is the worth of a person who chooses ignorance? Who indulges entirely in fear? What good can come of a person like that? Monkey no see, monkey no hear, monkey no speak.

I am actually shaking. I feel like how the especially crazy army people get about draft dodgers. Pussies. With pussies for pussies. Go away and leave this humanity business to those who can deal.

Every woman is afraid of childbirth, my mother recites, bored. *Also her mother's an idiot. The apple doesn't fall far. You know what your problem is?*

Fucking great, Janice. What's my problem?

Your problem is that you love all these girls so much more than they love you. You only want a woman you can save. Or one who can save you.

Avoiding pain will get you nowhere. Avoiding pain multiplies pain exponentially.

Good luck arguing that case.

One of the high school Lindsays, now a TV executive, posts pictures of her new baby with the nanny. The nanny cuddling the baby, the nanny kissing the baby, the nanny keeping watch in an armchair three feet from the sleeping baby. Physicists say energy is never lost, only transferred, transformed. I send a virtual thumbs-up, do my part for peace.

And what else? Looks like Molly got married. Photos appear. Guy is good-looking in a symmetrical sort of way. Wearing a gold Rolex, however, which on a man under eighty-five is patently absurd. He doesn't look very ironic. He looks like, here I am with my chosen bride; soon I will impregnate her and we will buy a lovely home and become more or less exactly like our parents, who are themselves quite marvelous. At least have the decency to be not quite so pleased with yourself, man.

Molly and her longed-for husband, into whose mouth she is here spooning wedding cake, here mocking the act of spooning wedding cake. It's all nice and traditional. Hotel ballroom. Molly! Who once sucked off two guys at once for the email address of the head writer of a long-running sitcom.

My posture's shitty, like I'm trying to get inside the screen. Then I really see her, right in front of my burning eyeballs.

She's wearing a wedding getup precisely, to the detail the same as mine. Exactly the same kind of bias cut and exactly the same kind of bolero jacket and exactly the same hair arrangement, pinned loosely back with a big orchid behind the left ear. She is done up exactly like me. Only all in white, like a proper bride.

• • •

Fine, I do hate women.

How original, my mother says.

They're so obedient, traitorous. Descendants of the ones who gave up other women as witches.

No argument here. She shrugs.

Women who choose friends more beautiful than they are, striving, basking in the glow. Women who seek out friends less beautiful than they are, to prop themselves up. The self-destructive ones, the ones who are even more self-destructive, the truly sick ones who the less self-destructive ones eventually abandon. The ones in hot pursuit, always, always, of a male, any male, that male, no, no, that one.

You have no trouble making friends. You make friends easy. It's keeping them you can't manage.

Because I don't like women.

They don't like you either, obviously.

The crazies trying to extend their fertility, taking hormones, slathering themselves with pureed money. It's like, yo, ladies, actually, guess what? Amazing news. You're pardoned! You're free! The prison gates are wide open. Go! You made bail! Get out, you've served your time, your sentence is over! Wear comfy shoes and clothes you can move in and Be a Person! Run free! Put on elastic-waist pants, learn how to do some useful things, read books, explore, think for yourself, live your liiiiiiiife!

The problem, sweetheart, is you.

But it's like with animals raised in captivity, the ones that can't ever acclimate back into nature? The ones who won't run away no matter how wide open the cage door.

It's true, my mother concedes. *You're not looking cute, ladies. Hair dye just makes you look like an old lady with dyed hair. Perfume makes you smell like you're deathly afraid of your body. Let it go. Give it up. Be aged, bitches. Be a body. It's happening anyway.*

The whole get-fucked-by-the-system-and-take-pills-and-lie-about-the-truth-of-your-life-until-you-die thing doesn't really appeal to me.

You just want to figure out how to wind up a happy old lady. That's it. How do you wind up a happy cogent confident content old lady? Friendly with gravity. Friends with your body.

We're all trying to outpace the same shit, but some of us won't admit it, some of us can't name it, and we call those women oppressed.

Why yes, Ariella, my mother says, prim and proper. *Quite a mystery that you cannot seem to maintain a friendship with a woman.*

You are the least dead dead person I've ever met.

I agree to accompany Mina to the co-op. Zev at six weeks old has plumped up real nice. He's changed in just the few days since I've seen him.

We sit in the café not talking.

Fine. Fine. Fine. Fine.

Not much sleep last night, Mina says, finally. I hate the way her lower lip protrudes. She thinks she's so great with her unwashed hair and her ancient boots and her mysterious absent baby daddy.

No ticky no laundry, I say. What the fuck? I didn't sleep so great either. A full moon, northeasterly blow. When you lose sleep, you lose your mind.

She is nursing Zev like gangbusters now, early snafu all cleared up. My services are no longer needed.

I don't know how to thank you, she keeps saying. *I just can't thank you enough.*

The more she says it, the more I hate her.

She hands me Zev and goes to the bathroom, and did you know it's almost impossible to feel aggression when you're holding an infant? A chemical thing. Farewell, little guy. This will be the last. I'm quick about it, just one last nip before she comes back. How calm it makes me.

Weirdly warm for January. All the snow from last week's storm already melted.

Last summer a giant two-hundred-year-old tree in the park was declared dead of beetle infestation and had to be removed in a process that took several days and lots of men shouting and a few big trucks. The beetles had thrived especially well after a not-too-cold winter. Someday another summer. I can't imagine sweating. Think of all the freshly dead trees there'll be. And in the summer you can't imagine shivering. In the dry years the people forget all about the wet years; in the wet years they forget all about the dry years. And Rose of Sharon, having given birth to a dead child, offers her full breasts to the starving man, who drinks and is saved.

Dear Marianne, I have decided once and for all to do my doctoral work on the interstices of traditional religion and worship of female power.

Mina reappears and takes Zev back.

She used you, my mother says.

We got it, Mina coos at him. He's windmilling his arms,

overjoyed. *Don't we, baby? Don't we got it? Oh yeah, we got it now, sweet boy. We got it all under control now. We're good to go now.*

So go, I say. *Bye.*

In the car in the Starbucks lot out by mall with sleeping Walker and Adrienne Rich. I'm not reading the Rich; I'm reading the Internet on my device, going blind and dumb. I have to pee.

Baby stirs. I panic. I should have taken off his coat and hat and gloves, but it was so cold when we got in. I watch him in the rearview. Fast asleep. Good. Crucial. The nap is everything. But oh my God do I have to pee.

Mina rings the bell. Nine thirty in the morning and I have no clue how I am going to fill my day.

I have something for you.

I stand in the doorway with hands on hips, scowling at her.

Can't we just skip the small talk?

It's an amber stone on a leather cord.

A nursing bead, she explains, tying it around my neck. Traditionally worn through the child's infancy, through teething, as a kind of attractive third nipple for the baby to play with, chew on, generally enjoy through its transitions.

We're like war buddies, she says. *We're in the shit together.*

Lives on the line. A gendered rite of passage.

The nursing bead is solid and strong in my palm. I squeeze it. *Thank you,* I croak.

You're welcome, she says.

I'm sorry, I say.

I know, she says. *C'mere. Poor baby.*

I move toward her and she wraps me up tight.

I am forgiven. For now.

Paul found fresh animal feces in the attic.

You have got to be kidding me, he says before falling into bed like a mighty felled tree.

I'll call Will, I say, secretly happy for the excuse.

Grrrrreat, Paul says into the pillow.

Any fool can see that he needs some attention, so I blow him. His perspective improves immediately, and he's out in seconds.

I get it, Ari, Will tells me in the morning, flat on his back with a flashlight in a corner of the attic. A flash of skin above his belt. His muscular belly, dusted with fine dark hair. *You know? I totally get it. I get not being interested in what's expected of you.*

Oh.

I mean, do you have any idea what a fuck-you to my father it was, becoming a fucking carpenter? To a man who wrote books about books about books? He was so disappointed. He was so let down.

Well, screw that. Putting your own ambition on your children. That sucks.

He sat up and grinned.

Walker's a lucky kid.

I roll my eyes.

Why can't we fall in love—true and deep—without it being some huge threat to the working order of things? In another life Will and I might rip each other's clothes off with our teeth and make a whole new world out of entirely different problems. But this is not that life, and I get that.

Falling in love often is crucial. You just have to let it nourish you without giving in to it. Why turn it off entirely? Why deaden any part of yourself? Won't death do that for you, and soon enough?

Jewish summer camp Jess once told me that hair holds a lot of energy.

I spread newspaper under me and sit before the floor-length mirror.

I hesitate. I am brave. I go at it. All of it.

Shorter than it's ever been. Feels amazing for about an hour. Gone, all of it. Walker claps and laughs and points and plays with the trimmings until the mess gets to be too much.

I love it, Paul says. All night I can't stop touching it. Walker keeps pointing at me, giggling madly. *Mama?* he says, looking around for me like I've disappeared, a game. *Mama? Mama! Mama!*

He's found me. I'm new.

By the time I wake up the next day it's completely awful, exposes my whole horrible face, nothing to hide behind, nothing pretty about me anymore, a disaster. Paul laughs.

I'm getting to know her better, this complicated ecosystem. I ply her with teas and aromas and offerings of peace, placate her, beseech her to leave me alone, leave me in peace. I'm scared of my power sometimes. Distinctly female. I should shave my legs one of these days. It's been months. I'm starting to look like I live in a cave. Not that Paul cares. Or will admit caring. Paul's wanting does not hinge on anything other than the fact of me. This is an excellent trait in a man. The bad haircut, for instance, changes things not a whit. The hideous scar, the changes Walker hath wrought. He does not demand manicures. I love Paul. One of the great pleasures of my life, he is.

Tonight I sing Walker the lullaby from *Three Men and a Baby.* It's the only lullaby I can think of. He fusses. Was I sung to? Surely I was. Must have been. Some anonymous Caribbean dirge, some South American love song. Some anonymous singer, her fat lips at my brow. Someone must have loved me, way back. Some unknown employee, holding me close. Away from her own children, loving me instead.

Good night, sweetheart, well, it's time to go (Do do do do). I looked it up once, and there's not much more to it than that. *Do do de do do de do do de do do.* Seems to work okay, given that he's asleep when I'm done.

Adrienne Rich had it right. No one gives a crap about motherhood unless they can profit off it. Women are expendable and the work of childbearing, done fully, done consciously, is all-consuming. So who's gonna write about it if everyone doing it is lost forever within it? You want adventures, you want poetry and art, you want to salon it up over at Gertrude and Alice's, you'd best leave the messy all-consuming baby stuff to someone else. Birthing and nursing and rocking and distracting and socializing and cooking and washing and gardening and mending: what's that compared with bullets whizzing overhead, dazzling destructive heroics, headlines, parties, glory, all that Martha Gellhorn stuff, all that Zelda Fitzgerald stuff, drugs and gutters and music and poetry pretty dresses more parties and fucking and fucking and parties?

Destroy yourself, says my mother. *Live it up. That's what makes for good stories.*

She should know.

Nurturance, on the other hand . . .

The time it takes to grow something . . .

BORING.

Crisp and Jer hosted a party for last year's visiting writer, a Dutch poet.

Come, Jer said. *Mothers need to party, too.* So I brought my tiny Walker bundle, and Paul helped me limp over there. What a gift: invited somewhere nice with my terrifying appendage.

The Dutch writer was sweet but standoffish. He spoke to me just once.

In Holland we have a saying, he said, gesturing at my bundle. *The Tropical Years. When the Dutch colonized Indonesia, you see, military service there counted for double time. Because you must understand it was terribly hot. And the malaria and the disease, and so forth. So it was that one year of military service in the tropics counted for two. Tropical years, it was called. This is what it is to have small children, you understand?*

We order pizza for her farewell dinner, open some red. I light candles, put on Dinosaur Jr.

Will declined my invitation. It occurs to me way too late: Will and Mina! She'll come visit. Brooklyn isn't far. Her sister will drive her bonkers, she'll come stay with us, she'll fall in love with Will, our little commune will be set.

Damn, girl, Mina says about my hair. *Damn.*

So sexuality's a continuum, says Bryan when we're eating.

Right. I'm game.

In the middle you have perfectly bisexual, on either end you have perfectly straight and perfectly gay.

Most of us are in the middle somewhere, Mina says.

Obviously. But my theory is that women have to be at the exact same place on the bisexuality continuum in order to be friends.

Say more.

If you veer toward gay but your friend veers toward straight, you're always going to want a more intense level of relationship, and she won't be that interested.

Yeah, Mina says, *like they're terrified you might just jump them and chow down on their pussy.*

I can't stop laughing. I'm good and tipsy. Paul goes up to bed. He can only take so much. It's only nine o'clock, but Paul is Paul and I love him and I get him and it's fine.

So wait. How gay am I?

Probably you're at, like, about seventy percent, and you—he turns to me—*are closer to fifty. Just off the top of my head.*

You wait until I have butch hair to tell me this?

Naw, me and Ari are the exact same amount of queer, Mina says. *The exact same. And we're in love.*

She's blushing. Look at her.

You guys. They just found a giant squid, I say.

What?

I watched a show about it. They found a giant squid. First ever. I mean, they've existed in mythology, but no one had ever actually caught one until now.

That's cool.

Well, yeah, this fishing boat way out in the deepest Atlantic catches this thing in these deep-sea nets by accident and they haul it up and they can't believe it because no one has ever been able to confirm the existence of these things.

Wow.

But what do they do once they've hauled it up in the deep-sea net, first time anyone's ever laid eyes on its kind?

They kill it.

Of course. Then they put it on ice and try to get it to a lab immediately so it can be cut up and studied and whatever.

Moral of the story?

Don't get caught?

Don't be interesting.

Let them mythologize you down there in the depths, let them wonder, but don't show yourself, for God's sake.

Maybe it wanted help.

There is no help.

What scares me late at night is that Walker's a *person;* he hears what I say and looks up at me and wants to love me but doesn't yet have any clue how fucked up I am. Here he is, we brought him here, he's one of us now, the living. It's pretty simple: an infant is to be held and bundled up and carried around. Fed, tended, protected. Helpless creature. You learn to humble yourself to him, pie-faced god. And you want to feel the enormity of that? Want it to hit you square? Imagine him hurt. Imagine him suffering. Imagine him taken. Imagine him dead. Imagine your arms empty. Imagine it, imagine it, imagine it.

These tiny people, they're not about you. They are not for you. They do not belong to you. They are under your care, is all, and it's your job to work at being a decent human being, love them well and a lot, don't put your problems on them, don't make your problems their problems, don't use them to occupy empty parts of yourself.

So you're finally growing up, my mother says, standing behind me at the sink while I get started on the dishes. I feel aged. My body says no. I think I might see her reflection if I look up at the darkened window, but it's so fogged up that I can't even see myself.

Yeah, I guess, I tell her, so she'll leave me alone. I'm too tired to fight, and I'll do whatever I have to do to spare the child my weaknesses and faults. Swear that if he winds up broken, it will not be by me.

Pain-in-the-ass bank snafu error message; I'm supposed to call them and straighten it out.

Mother's maiden name?

I hesitate, as though saying it might summon her. As though saying it might rouse her from tenuous slumber.

Hello?

Um.

Hello?

Walker, Paul said. *How about Walker?*

Walker?

You know, like Walker Percy, Walker Evans.

I called it up on my device.

It means cloth washer. It's Old English. In the medieval era, workers trod on wool to cleanse it of impurities.

There's something kind of nice about that, don't you think?

Yeah. I mean, maybe. But don't you think it's weird to reach into Old English for a name?

Why?

I'm Jewish. You're whatever you are. What are you again?

Whatever.

No, seriously, remind me?

Way back Scottish. Some Italian.

Right, so you're whatever, I'm a Jew. And he'll be a Jew, technically.

Technically.

Yeah, well, technically's pretty much all that counts with the Jews. A technicality-loving folk.

So you want something Hebrew-y? Old Testament style?

I didn't say that.

Good. Because that would be weird, too.

I like Walker. I like what it's about. And walking. Walking's the best.

How about Biker? Bikes are pretty great.

Be serious.

Oh. Okay. Is there a rule about that?

No.

Okay. Let's see . . . Janice-for-a-boy?

Are you serious?

No. Cal. Clement.

Carl.

Cory.

God, they're all so bad. Why do all names sound so dumb?

You remember that Seinfeld *bit about having to hurry up and have kids because by the time you're forty you've met someone you dislike with every name in existence?*

Yeah, so it's down to, like, Calyx.

I never met a Calyx I didn't love.

Corinthian.

Corrado.

Cantonese.

Catatonic.

Come Hither.

Caaaah-razy.

Two dreams.

One. A faint, steady wail coming from somewhere inside the wall at the back of my closet.

Crap, what now. Did the raccoon have babies? A family of bats?

Will comes over.

I'm convinced it's a baby, I say. He stands very still, listening to the steady wail.

It's a baby. We'll have to open up the wall.

I nod. But first, can't resist. He lowers me into a chair and I am pliant, warm. Hang on a minute, baby. Then the wailing stops.

Silence. I'm alone. I begin to tear through the wall, smash through. There's a small passageway and an opening. The wailing has stopped. The baby is dead. The baby was hungry. The baby starved. The baby gave up. The baby is dead. Paul comforts me.

Two. I'm pregnant. I am terribly upset. Beyond hysterical. I will procure an abortion immediately!

I'm looking up the number and dialing and pressing 4 for more information and waiting on hold while the bullshit music plays and I start to count the months. August, it'll be. Everything hot and lush, nights in short sleeves. A new girl, fresh and soft and naked on my chest.

How smart she'll be. How free. Open and kind. Happy, secure. She won't sneak a peek at herself when passing any reflective surface. Rarely threatened. Know what she deserves.

One day she'll grow gray. Rarely paint her face. Eat slowly, move her body often, all sweat and love. Do as she pleases, disregard the superficial, listen more than she talks, stay calm. Be good to herself. Make things. Fix things. Grow things.

Finally someone picks up.

Hello?

I will be her shining example. I'll become it, so as to never let her down.

Anyone? Anyone? Bueller?

And oh yeah. And I'll give birth to her. Do the work, earn her. No avoiding the pain, but I can't wait to make its acquaintance, see its face, square with it. Exciting. What is pain if you don't suffer it? I will make myself worthy.

Harlan, is that you? Listen, I told you I was going to report you if you called more than twice a day. Harlan, are you taking your meds? You know I have to call your caseworker if you harass us, Harlan.

I hang up. Smash the phone down on the receiver. Old-fashioned receiver, beige.

We'll do it together—me and this baby girl. She'll be here in the dog days of summer. We'll claw our way grunting screaming moaning ecstatically toward each other. A girl.

And if I die trying? If we both do??

Fine.

Cold. More snow. It is never going to end, this winter. Ice. Twelve degrees Fahrenheit.

People don't remember what winter used to be like, says Didi at the co-op. *You'd have the first snow either before or after Christmas, and then it would snow until March. There would always be snow on the ground. My kids don't understand why there's so much snow this year. This is normal. What's weird is how little snow there's been in the last few years.*

We're in the deli, packing and pricing millet salad and sweet-potato-bakes half quarts. Walker's asleep on my back.

A beautiful little family comes walking up to the case, browsing the sandwiches. Pretty mommy, hair shiny, sweet face, baby in a sling on her chest. Maybe seven months old, the perfect age, no longer so terrifyingly easy to kill, but not exerting any of that annoying independence just yet. They look calm and proud, connected, a team. The mom has found her balance. Or maybe she never lost it in the first place. Maybe it's all been okay for her. But I tend to doubt it.

Kabuki Face from Paul's department comes in just before the end of my shift. Haven't seen her since the faculty party in November. I decide not to ignore her. It takes so little in the beginning: a moment of eye contact, an exchange, laying down of arms, and an agreement: women agree to be friends, or to be friend*ly,* until one of them crosses a line, decides she doesn't so much like the other after all, and then the friendship, or the friendliness, is over. Sometimes it takes minutes, sometimes it takes years.

How's it going?

Good, good, she says. *And you?*

I shrug. *Okay.*

Are you? She actually seems to want to know.

Yeah, I say unconvincingly. *You know.* But she sees through me.

It's hard, she says.

Yeah.

I had a really bad time of it.

You did?

God. Yeah. Long time ago. They're twenty-two and nineteen now.

She's kind of a badass; I never saw it before. Fidelity to that kind of aesthetic requires real toughness. She brushes a piece of hair out of my eyes. Dare I call it maternal? Her hand is cool and dry. Her eyes are not unkind. Damn, she is unafraid. I find nothing to say.

She smiles, pushes her cart onward and around to the next aisle.

See you, she calls back over her shoulder.

And I don't hate her. I don't have a problem with her at all. She's fine by me. So maybe I'm better.

ACKNOWLEDGMENTS

The line "A person who doesn't have friends must explain herself to strangers" is from the poem *Midwinter Day* by Bernadette Mayer, copyright © 1982 by Bernadette Miller and published by New Directions.

The line "Pay attention to what they tell you to forget" is from Muriel Rukeyser's poem "Double Ode," copyright ©1976 by Muriel Rukeyser. It can be found in *Home/Birth: A Poemic* by Arielle Greenberg and Rachel Zucker, copyright © 2010 and published by 1913 Press.

My parents, Elissa Blaser, Katharine Noel, Nalini Jones, Ike Herschkopf, Amy Griffin, Binnie Kirshenbaum, Miranda Beverly-Whittemore, Allison Oberhand, Jessica Cherry, Amy Webb, Thea Carlson, Heather Samples, Hawa Allan, Rebecca Wolff, Brin Quell, Madhavi Tandon Batliboi, Elanit Weisbaum, Ann Wolf, Bill and Carol Schwarzschild, Heidi Factor, Margaret Wimberger, Emily Andrukaitis, Laura Gianino,

Carla Gray, Hannah Harlow, and everyone at HMH, Poppy Hampson and everyone at Chatto and Windus, DTV Germany, Niew Amsterdam, The College of Saint Rose, Columbia University School of the Arts, Djerassi, Virginia Center for the Creative Arts, the Netherlands Institute for Advanced Study, and more or less everyone I know: thank you for inspiration, sustenance, and support of all kinds while I worked to bring this book into being. Thank you Writers House, thank you Simon Lipskar—you are the man. Thank you Lauren Wein: editor, book doula, *chevruta*. Thank you Ed, my love, and Miller D, our love.